DEATH IN THE DEPTHS

Eric listened to the seven pairs of boots sloshing in the water just a few feet from where he was submerged. Tiny air bubbles squeezed out of his nose. He was losing it.

All of a sudden the boots began moving away. Hold on a little longer, he told himself. His head throbbed and, when he closed his eyes, he saw little popping lights. Suddenly, his chest heaved, desperate for air. He sucked in a stream of dirty water through his mouth. He gagged, his head jerking as it choked out some of the rancid water, swallowing some. If only he could hold on a few more seconds. Just a few more.

It was no use. His chest spasmed again, water plunged into his mouth. Gripping his crossbow, he broke for the surface. . . .

THE WARLORD
By Jason Frost

THE WARLORD (1189, $3.50)
The world's gone mad with disruption. Isolated from help, the survivors face a state in which law is a memory and violence is the rule. Only one man is fit to lead the people, a man raised among the Indians and trained by the Marines. He is Erik Ravensmith, THE WARLORD—a deadly adversary and a hero of our times.

#2: THE CUTTHROAT (1308, $2.50)
Though death sails the Sea of Los Angeles, there is only one man who will fight to save what is left of California's ravaged paradise. His name is THE WARLORD—and he won't stop until the job is done!

#3: BADLAND (1437, $2.50)
His son has been kidnapped by his worst enemy and THE WARLORD must fight a pack of killers to free him. Getting close enough to grab the boy will be nearly impossible—but then so is living in this tortured world!

#4: PRISONLAND (1506, $2.50)
Former inmates of San Quentin rule the ruins of San Francisco! When a small group of courageous women on the island fortress of Alcatraz makes a stand against the brutal reign of terror, there's only one man brave enough to lead them—THE WARLORD!

BADLAND
THE WARLORD

#3

BY JASON FROST

ZEBRA BOOKS
KENSINGTON PUBLISHING CORP.

ZEBRA BOOKS

are published by

Kensington Publishing Corp.
475 Park Avenue South
New York, N.Y. 10016

Second printing: October 1985

Printed in the United States of America

To Ramona Van Dyck,
who keeps the Warlord from losing his crossbow.

Book One:

THE MEANS OF EVIL

Who overcomes
By force hath overcome but half his foe.
                                        —Milton

1.

It was dark. Which was the only thing keeping Eric Ravensmith alive. That and the three feet of filthy swamp water covering his exhausted body.

He hugged the heavy flat rock to his chest to keep him from floating up to the surface. His cheeks were puffed out with stored air like a bullfrog's as he squirmed his shoulder blades deeper into the muddy creek bottom. Christ, it was cold. His teeth ached. His toes were already numb inside his soggy Nike running shoes. His fingers weren't much better. He tried to scratch his thigh where the thorns had shredded his pants and skin, but his icy fingers kept stabbing the wrong place. Finally he gave up and just waited.

Six feet away, the sloshing of heavy combat boots. There were eight men now, wading hip-deep through the icy water. All armed. All after him. Dirk Fallows's renegade soldiers.

"Hey, guys, hold it a minute," one of them called.

"Hold this, Greene," someone answered. Rough laughter.

The voices sifted down through the water to Eric as if having first passed through several thick doors. But he could still make out the words.

"He went through here. Right here. I saw him."

"Well, he ain't fucking here now, Greene."

"He was. Running with that damned crossbow of his. Right through here."

"Uh-huh. Sure."

"Fuck you, Dobbs."

Dobbs laughed. "Your mama beat you to it, sonny. She's comin' back tonight for sloppy seconds. Yum, yum."

"Shut your—"

"Let's just spray the whole creek with bullets," someone else suggested. "If he's here, that'll finish him."

"Yeah, right." Dobbs again, that cocky twang in his voice daring somebody, anybody, to disagree. "Then you can tell Fallows how you used up all his bullets. Man, he'd rather chew through your throat with his bare teeth than waste one fuckin' bullet."

"Got that right," someone agreed.

"'Sides, he said to capture the bastard alive if possible."

"That's what I mean," Greene said. "It ain't possible. Son of a bitch is good, man. Real good."

Jesus, Eric thought, why couldn't they argue while they kept walking? How long had he been underwater now? One minute? Two? It felt longer.

At first his lungs had just tickled. Now they burned. Like the first time he'd tried to smoke a cigarette, he and Billy One-Nation in the boy's room after geography. Eighth grade. Unfiltered Camel. The raw raking feeling in his throat just before the principal caught them. Three whacks each.

"Look, if he's dumb enough to be hunkering in this ice water, all we gotta do is stand around and wait for him to come to the surface. He can't hold his breath forever."

"Brilliant, Ryan. Fuckin' genius, man. Only what if Greene's wrong and the asshole is already half a mile ahead of us? We sit around here with our thumbs up our asses and he's laughing knowing what Fallows is gonna do to us if we go back empty-handed."

Eric opened his eyes and stared up toward the surface. He saw only the dark, filthy water, backed by dark, moonless sky. He could just as well be staring down into some bottomless cavern. Not at all like when he was a kid lying at the bottom of the community pool, seeing how long he could hold his breath while he watched the girls and their skinny frog legs kicking overhead. Old enough to like watching them, too young to know why. Finding out why didn't come until the next summer.

The heavy boots churned closer to him, maybe

three feet away. They were heading straight for him. He reached out his hand, groping through the mud for his Barnett Commando crossbow, already cocked and fitted with a sharp bolt.

"OK," Greene said. The movement stopped. "I got an idea. We go over there and stand shoulder-to-shoulder from one side of the creek to the other. Then we just walk up the creek until we find him. Like a human net. Whatya think?"

Dobbs said, "I think you're a fuckin' idiot, Greene. What makes you think he's in the water?"

"'Cause I saw him splashing through here, but I didn't see him come out. That's why."

"You didn't see him come out, huh?"

"No, I didn't." Defiant.

"Tough shit. We're not marching through this whole damn river just 'cause you don't see so good. Fallows told us this guy was some kind of hotshot soldier, served with him back in 'Nam. In that spook outfit, uh, Night Shift."

"He's an Indian, too," someone else said.

"Nah, just brought up near 'em, Fallows said. Still, he knows some of their shit. Tracking and stuff."

"So?" Greene said.

"So, I'm sayin' maybe you didn't see Ravensmith because you're too fuckin' stupid or he's too fuckin' good. Take your choice. Only I ain't standing around ass-deep in this frozen piss water while you figure it out. I say we fan out with Darby at point and Ryan and Phelps on the flanks. And we comb through this brush like a whore looking for her virginity till we found his ass. Then we kick it the hell back to Fallows. That's what I say. What do you say, Greene Bean?" There it was, the challenge.

Eric's lungs started to clench, trying to breathe despite him. Only his willpower kept them from sucking in the muddy water. But even that was getting harder to exert. Willpower was one thing, but breathing was a whole different story. His skull felt awkward, like a too-tight helmet. He could almost feel his brain expanding, swelling and contracting under his scalp as it panicked for air. Soon he'd *have* to breathe. Or drown.

Above him and three feet to the right he could picture the two men facing each other, Greene and Dobbs, their sweaty hands on their weapons, their mean eyes locked. Thinking, what if I'm first on the trigger? The others would be casually backing off now, anxious to see who would win, but not wanting to be in the way of any stray bullets if it came to that. Sometimes it did.

Finally, Eric heard Greene's voice, a little sheepish, but still trying to sound hard like he'd made up his own mind. "Fallows said you were in charge, Dobbs, so we follow you. For now."

"Bet your ass you do, sucker. OK, let's hump on over to the shore, start fingering through these weeds. Greene, you're so fond of the water, I want you to stay in the creek, following us north. You see anything swimming around that ain't got fins, you give a holler. Got it?"

"Yeah, Dobbs, I got it."

Eric listened to seven pairs of boots sloshing to the shore, knowing that one pair still stood nearby. Damn! He twisted his head to the side, hoping to at least catch a glimpse of Greene, pinpoint his location. But it was no use. There was nothing to see. Only black, gritty water brushing against his eyes like sandpaper.

He clutched the rock tighter to his chest, squeezing it as if to absorb any oxygen it might have. He tried not to think. Clear his mind. A crazy image persisted, banged his brain like a locomotive. There was Julie Andrews rushing over a green mountain, singing, "The hills are alive with the sound of music." Her cheeks were red from the crisp mountain air. Tons of it. She took deep breaths, winked at him.

Eric chuckled like a drunk. Tiny air bubbles squeezed out of his nose. He was losing it.

He heard Greene's boots starting to move away. Hold on a little longer. Think of something else.

Three lousy feet of water. Most shark attacks occur in three feet of water. Where'd he learn that? Of course, Timmy. Taking his son to see *Jaws* had resulted in the family having to listen to shark trivia for two weeks afterwards. Now the family was gone. His wife and daughter murdered. His son kidnapped. All by the same man. Dirk Fallows.

Eric dug his hand deep into the slimy mud next to him to warm his fingers. His head throbbed. He closed his eyes and saw little popping lights. Suddenly his chest heaved, desperate for air. He sucked in a stream of dirty water through his mouth. He gagged, his head jerking as it choked out some of the rancid water, swallowing some. Immediately he flattened himself into the mud again, hoping his movements hadn't noticeably disturbed the water's surface. Hadn't attracted attention.

He could no longer hear Greene's boots stomping through the mud and water. Was he gone, or only standing still, searching? He might even be staring at Eric right now. If only he could hold on a few more seconds. Just a few more.

It was no use. His chest spasmed again, water plunged into his mouth. He broke for the surface.

2.

Stanley Greene hated water. Always had. Always would.

There was no reason he could think of why he should hate water, no childhood trauma. He'd never nearly drowned, nor had anybody he'd known. In prison, they'd asked him about that because of that incident his first day when he'd refused to take a shower with the other inmates. The real reason was because Jesus Perez, who was doing three to five for armed robbery, had found out Stanley had slept with his girlfriend Maria the day after Jesus had been sent up. Now Jesus said he was going to do the same things to Stanley that Stanley had done to Maria. The skinny spic wasn't kidding, either. Of course, Stanley didn't tell the officials that. Instead he'd made up some story about having nightmares of being eaten alive by piranha. Yeah, piranhas, he'd told them, acting real scared, little fish with a lotta teeth snapping at his, uh, *thing*. He figured they'd like the sex angle. Actually, he'd gotten the idea from some jungle movie he'd seen on TV the day before his arrest. Something starring Johnny Weissmuller, but not as Tarzan. That had kept the shrinks busy scratching their heads for the eighteen months he'd done at Chino. Every so often they'd ask him about the nightmares, kinda offhand, like they'd just remembered, and he'd say, Yes, sir, they're worse than ever. Most every night now. Can't hardly sleep worrying about my thing.

Meantime, Jesus got a sharpened spoon through his right lung during a Johnny Cash concert. Bled to death in his seat right in the middle of "Amazing Grace." They never found out who did it. Stanley still had the spoon, wore it around his neck on a gold chain he'd swiped from Maria.

Stanley Greene never went swimming and, even without Jesus around, wasn't all that fond of showers or baths. Even before the quakes, when he was living with some buddies down near the beach in Venice, he'd get off work from the dry cleaners and walk along the beach only on the off chance that some cute high school chick in one of those skimpy string bikini jobs might start talking to him. He had a nice body himself that looked good in a tight bathing suit, but that damn suit

17

never once got wet since he'd owned it. Not once.

Water. Hell, he didn't even like to drink the stuff.

So what was he doing marching through this stinking creek in the middle of the night? That bastard Dobbs. Thought he was hot shit because Fallows put him in charge of this patrol. He'd go along because anything was better than having Fallows pissed at you. Jeez, this was the nastiest bunch of guys he'd ever seen brought together, in or out of prison, and they were all scared of Dirk Fallows. Still, that Dobbs had mouthed off a bit too much. Maybe could use some of Dr. Greene's spoon therapy. An attitude adjustment, yeah, between the ribs. Tickle, tickle, little Dobbs. Well, Stanley had seen what he'd seen. Ravensmith running through this creek, disappearing behind some brush, but not coming out on the other side. He'd seen it clearly through his scope.

But, then, where was the son of a bitch hiding?

Damn, this water was cold. Smelled bad, too. Probably being used as a toilet by most of the people living around here. Probably used it himself once or twice further upstream. Thinking about it now made him want to take a leak. He could just climb out for a second and take a whiz over in the bushes. Ah, what the hell, his pants were already wet. They'd need to be washed out after walking through this muck anyway. He stood still, cradled his M-16, and let himself go. The warmth felt kinda nice.

Then he heard something behind him. Something stirring in the water. He shouldered the M-16 as he spun to face it, his finger hooking around the trigger.

"Hey, Dobbs! Goddamn," Greene shouted, aiming his M-16 at Eric's emerging face. Jeez, that scar. *"Dobbs!"*

But Eric hadn't come up empty-handed. He'd brushed aside the heavy rock on his chest and snagged his crossbow on the way up, wedging the black metal stock to his shoulder as he popped through the surface and balanced on one knee. The hardest part had been squeezing the trigger before gulping down any air. But he hadn't wanted to spoil his aim. The bowstring catapulted the sharp wooden shaft with 175 pounds of fury.

The bolt plunged through Greene's chest, just below the sternum, punching out hunks of flesh and muscle and organs like coring an apple. The bloody bits splashed into the water behind him. A hungry gray fish surfaced, slurped up a chunk and dove back down.

Greene continued to stand there aiming at Eric a few seconds afterwards. Then he got a funny look on his face, as if he'd just remembered a song title he'd been struggling with for days. He looked down at the feathers sticking out of his chest, then flopped backwards into the water.

The metallic chatter of another M-16 echoed through the night and a spray of bullets stitched the water six inches in front of Eric. He sprang up and kicked through the water for the opposite shore.

Another burst of semiautomatic fire chewed up a branch of the tree just as Eric ducked behind it. Wood and leaf confetti sprinkled down onto his dripping head.

"Don't waste the bullets, you dinks!" Dobbs hollered. "Phelps, swing left. Hey, Ryan."

"Yeah?"

"How many grenades you got left?"

"Three."

"Loosen up your arm. You're pitching big league tonight."

Eric didn't move. They wanted to spook him, scare him into running so they could corner him. He hung the crossbow over his shoulder and pulled his Walther P.38 from his boot. He'd traded his Remington .32 for this. The man he'd traded with had been a hard bargainer, an ex-Honda salesman who applied a little too much pressure when he shook hands, trying to squeeze sincerity through your pores. He'd wanted Eric's Remington, the boxes of ammo, Tracy's Smith & Wesson .357 Combat Magnum and a night with Tracy, though he'd winked at Eric and said it wouldn't take a whole night, if Eric caught his drift. Eric did. The ex-Honda salesman had finally settled for the Remington, the ammo, half a jar of Skippy extra-crunchy peanut butter and a broken hand.

Eric wasn't worried about the Walther. He could've buried it at the bottom of the creek and dug it up a week later and chances were it would still clip the ears off a squirrel with the first shot. The pull on these things was a little rough, like squeezing a grapefruit, but it still delivered.

He jammed the gun into the waist of his pants, recocked the crossbow, and slid a bolt into the brass runner. It was too dark for them to be certain of where he was, so they were trying to force him to make a move, give himself away. If he fired his gun, they'd have the flash to zero in on. With the crossbow, they'd see nothing.

To his left, maybe thirty feet. A noise. The squeak of feet moving in wet boots. It was faint, could almost be mistaken for the sound of some anxious bird. Probably just what the guy hoped. But Eric had spent a lot of his youth learning the difference, mostly in front of a TV screen in Big Bill Tenderwolf's house on the Hopi reservation.

"Christ, listen to that, would ya?" Big Bill would say, pointing his beer can at the TV and shaking his head. They'd be watching another one of those cowboy and Indian cheapies. "Hear that noise? They're trying to tell us that that's how the Apaches communicate. Jesus, sounds more like someone farting than a bird calling." Then he'd let go with some warbling that always made Eric smile. "Now *that's* what a fucking owl sounds like."

Eric stood shivering in the dark, waiting for the squeaking to get closer, lifting his crossbow, following the sound with the point of his arrow.

Squeak.

Squeak.

Whoosh.

The bolt zipped through the brush, rustling leaves as it spit into the night, finally chipping the edge of a pine tree and sticking in the ground.

Eric immediately dropped to the ground. He hadn't really expected to hit anybody, but he had expected something else. It came.

A blast from somebody's pistol, a 9mm from the sound of it, maybe a Steyer GB or a Tarus PT-99. Eric could see the flash only twenty feet away, hear the slug whizzing overhead on its way to the creek.

Less than two seconds after the shot, half a dozen other shots drummed the air. All of them directed at the flash twenty feet to the left of Eric. As he'd hoped.

"Stop it, goddamn it!" Dobbs yelled. "What the fuck you doing? Kriegstern? Hey, Kriegstern?" There was no answer. "Nice work, morons. You just blasted Kriegstern. Remember him? He's the guy with the wart on his eyelid. Worst fucking poker player in the squad. You killed him with me still holding his markers worth eight cartons of cigarettes and fifty rounds of ammo. Christ."

Eric crawled behind another tree. He'd been tempted to go after Kriegstern's body, see what provisions he might scavenge. If nothing else, that 9mm would come in handy. But they'd be expecting that. They'd be waiting.

Absently, Eric pinched at the thin, white scar that clung to his jawline before dripping down his

22

neck like hot wax. Another memento from Dirk Fallows.

OK, get organized, Eric. First thing to do is hotfoot it back to Tracy, who he'd left to make camp just outside Santa Carlotta. Or what was left of Santa Carlotta. Wait here, he'd told her, I'm just going to scout their camp. Nothing more. She'd nodded, told him to be careful, she'd seen a cougar earlier when she'd gathered wood. He'd known she was lying, but had agreed to be extra careful. That was one of the strange things about Tracy. Lately, maybe in the last month, she'd started lying. Not about anything serious, not in a malicious way. About small things, things he'd usually know were lies anyway. But she'd say them with a straight face and argue like hell if he challenged her. At first it had bothered him. Now it was almost like a game, a charming game that somehow enhanced their intimacy. Like with the cougar story, he could tell she'd been disappointed when he hadn't challenged her about it, so right before he left he'd asked her exactly where she'd seen this cougar. She'd pointed south.

"That's south. We came in from the west."

She pointed west. "Right. I meant there."

"Uh-huh. There haven't been any cougars there in years. They moved north toward the mountains."

"They must be making a comeback."

He gave her a look.

She bristled. "Hey, Eric, you don't have to live with the fucking Hopi Indians to know a cougar

23

when you see one. Big tail, pointed ears, claws the size of garden rakes. Yeah, it's a cougar."

"They're called pumas, not cougars."

"Whatever. Still rip your heart out."

He nodded and she gave him a triumphant smile.

"I'm just going for a quick look around. Be back in an hour."

That was four hours ago.

Eric had circled Fallows's camp, counting men, studying defenses, etching a mental map into his brain. Everything according to plan. Until he'd seen Timmy.

He'd had to get closer. Timmy's thirteenth birthday had been last week. The first birthday Eric hadn't been with him. Now, after three months as the captive of the man who'd butchered his mother and sister, Timmy was standing only a hundred yards away.

Eric was tempted to just dash in, grab the boy and run out again. But he knew they'd both be cut down within seconds. He had to swallow his emotion, jam it back somewhere deep inside where it wouldn't interfere.

But looking at Timmy touched something he couldn't protect. The boy's face was pale, the eyes dark, hollow. Not from malnutrition. If anything he'd even gained weight. But there was something in the walk, a bit of a swagger now. And the mouth, pressed into a mean sneer. Gone was the gentleness in the eyes, the quick smile, the whooping laugh of his mother. Instead he was starting to resemble the cruel soldiers he was living among. My God, starting to look a little like Dirk Fallows.

Eric struggled to think of some way to get a message to Timmy, some warning to be ready. At least assure him that Eric hadn't forgotten him. But there was no safe way.

Eric watched from the brush, suddenly startled by a drop on his cheek. Immediately he looked up, fearing rain, but realizing with some surprise it was his own tears. He hadn't shed a single tear since Annie's and Jenny's deaths. Had tried to kill that part of him, that feeling part, until Timmy was freed. But there it was anyway. damn.

They'd spotted him almost by accident. Three of Fallows's troops were chasing one of the girls they'd bought the day before from some rough-neck camp. The girl was maybe twenty-three, twenty pounds overweight, with short, stringy hair. Naked. She ran, waddled really, through the woods, thorny branches clawing her pale skin raw. The men ran after her, laughing and squealing like pigs. One of them had her panties stretched over his Padres baseball cap, the leg openings hooked around his ears.

"Here, sweetie," he yelled. "Oink, oink."

She kept running, her mouth open and gasping for air, her chubby legs wobbly. Finally she collapsed into the dirt.

The three men stood around her laughing. The one with the panties on his head reached down, pinched one of her nipples, and yanked her by the nipple to her feet.

"P-please," she sobbed. "Please."

One of them grinned. "Christ, Roy, she's beggin' for it. Beggin'."

"Well, now, I told you I had a way with women. I guess she ain't never known somebody with as much imagination as me. Hell, 'tween the three of us, we showed her more combinations than a fuckin' bank vault." He tugged the bill of his cap lower. "Hey, honey, you ever see that movie *Deliverance*?"

"W-what?"

He twisted her nipple hard and she screamed. "*Deliverance*, you fat sow."

"I saw it, Roy," one of the others said. "Burt Reynolds. Son of a bitch can act."

"Well, there's a scene in there we're gonna act out right here, just the four of us. Right, fatty?" He twisted her nipple again.

"Yes! Yes!"

He smiled. "Good. Now get down on your knees like a good little sow."

She was sobbing hysterically now.

Roy jabbed his shotgun butt into her flabby stomach and she doubled over, grabbing her stomach as she dropped to her knees, sobbing. Mucus puffed from her nostrils.

"Yccch. You really are a pig." Roy handed his shotgun to one of the others and began unfastening his pants, pulling them down over his hips. He wore no underwear and his skin was even paler than the girl's, but with red sores all over his buttocks.

Eric watched, breathing silently through his mouth. This really had nothing to do with him. He was here for one thing, to get Timmy. Anything he might do to help that girl would only risk his life and therefore Timmy's. That was unacceptable. Besides, whatever happens would have happened anyway.

Roy let his pants puddle around his ankles while he hopped closer to the sobbing girl. He took off his hat and whacked her twice across her naked backside. "Quit moving, damn it!" He handed his hat to the same guy holding his shotgun. "Here, Greene. I always take my hat off in the presence of a lady."

"You got real manners, Roy," the other guy said.

"Dobbs, I got manners up the wazoo. Come here, you fat little watermelon. Quit yer bawlin'."

There was a sudden tearing sound, like a zipper being opened too fast. Then Roy yelled, spun around, his eyes huge with pain and fear. The crossbow bolt had drilled through his lower back, scraping his spinal column, severing a few important nerves on the way, and poked out of his abdomen a few inches below his navel. Roy staggered a couple steps, gaping at the bloody tip as if it were an alien invader. Then he grabbed the tip with both hands and pulled it all the way through his body. "Bastard!" he cried, staggering toward Eric on shaky legs, kicking at the pants around his ankles, holding the dripping arrow over his head like a spear. "I'll . . . kill . . . you." He pitched face forward into a thorny bush. Dead.

Greene and Dobbs didn't hesitate. They began hollering for others from camp, dropping to the ground as they aimed their weapons. Stanley Greene pumped a few twelve-gauge rounds at the tree Eric had been hiding behind, but by then Eric was gone.

And they were on his trail.

Now it was dark, and Eric was soaking. He folded a green leaf in his mouth to muffle his chattering teeth. He'd killed one, and they'd killed one, but there were six left. And at least three hand grenades.

He had to move slowly, stay alert. These guys weren't amateurs. Most had military backgrounds, a few were ex-cops. All had been trained by Dirk Fallows, and that was the most dangerous part of all.

Eric twisted through the brush, toeing aside crispy leaves and twigs, ducking branches. Each movement had to be carefully choreographed, each muscle disciplined to move with painful slowness. There was no room for error, no place for impatience. Only the right moves. The kind of moves that had kept him alive in 'Nam.

When he stood still, he could hear a faint rustling or a distant snap. He smiled grimly. The distance between them was increasing. With any luck, he might even be able to dodge them altogether before he gathered up Tracy.

Once he made it through the woods, there was a field of grass that curved over the hill toward Santa Carlotta. Immediately to the west was a jagged ridge with a forty-foot drop that formed the new coastline of California. The old one, originally two miles further west, was now underwater.

Eric studied the sky. No point in trying to read stars. The Long Beach Halo that domed the island of California seemed thicker than usual tonight. There was a pale smudge overhead, that would be the moon. But it offered no light. The Halo was like an overly protective parent tonight. Lights out and early to bed.

Eric crouched low and scrambled across the field, moving with such easy grace that he barely ruffled the long grass. His black crossbow was clutched in both hands, ready.

It wasn't too far to Tracy's camp now and he was sure he'd increased the margin between Fallows's men and him. But he was also sure they'd spot his tracks through the grass and follow. He knew how bad Fallows wanted him.

He ran faster, still keeping his head down, but only in a half crouch now, his legs thrashing through the field like a tractor.

He was moving so fast he almost missed it. That noise. Someone walking. Someone *in front*.

He lifted the crossbow as he straightened, his finger tightening against the trigger.

Until he felt the gun barrel thrust against his cheek.

"Oh, it's you," Tracy said, grinning. "I thought you were a puma."

*   *   *

The first grenade exploded about twenty-five feet away.

Tracy and Eric were knocked to the ground but were otherwise undamaged.

Tracy stirred, lifting her head and brushing the clods of dirt from her hair. "What the—"

"Visitors," Eric explained, pulling her to her feet.

They ran without looking back. Tracy's usual limp was hardly noticeable now. Twice they heard the metallic stuttering of semiautomatic firing, but the bullets plowed harmlessly through the field.

Then they heard Dobbs screaming. "Next asshole wastes bullets I'm gonna fucking kill myself!"

At the edge of the field, Tracy tripped over a rusty irrigation pipe, rolled forward and was back on her feet and running without missing a beat.

"Nice," Eric said.

"I was on the '80 Olympics gymnastic team. Broke my heart when we couldn't go to Moscow. Didn't I mention it?"

Eric shook his head as he ran. Christ. But he couldn't help smiling.

"There's a road through there." Tracy pointed. "When you didn't come back, I followed it to come looking for you."

"Where's it go?"

"I dunno. Into town I think."

"We'll find out."

They slid down the embankment to the road, a

30

narrow two-lane strip with most of the blacktop split and crumbled where the road had buckled during the quakes.

"Careful," he said as they hopped and dodged the huge chunks of macadam. Eric noticed that plants had already started growing in the highway's holes. In a year or two, the road would be completely grown over.

Tracy tapped him on the shoulder and nodded at the road sign. SANTA CARLOTTA, 2 MILES.

"You make it?" he asked, nodding at her bad hip.

"A cinch."

They fell into a rhythmic jogging pattern, making about seven minute miles. Occasionally Tracy would lag a step or two, but then she'd churn her arms and be right back up with him. She kept her mouth clenched and forced herself to keep breathing through her nose, just the way he'd taught her. When they'd first started out together in search of Timmy, she'd hardly been able to walk two miles without frequent rests. Then she'd been shot in the hip by that pirate, Rhino, leaving her with a limp. At first she'd needed a cane. Now she was running ten or twenty miles at a clip. And on the really long runs, if the pace was slow enough, she had better endurance than Eric. It didn't bother Eric. He was proud of her.

They could hear the clomping of the six pairs of combat boots crunching along behind them, maybe a half mile away. Fortunately the road was wooded on both sides and curvy enough to keep them from having a clear shot. The darkness helped, too.

Directly ahead, the modest storefronts and one-story homes began to appear in their neat little rows.

"Hometown, USA," Tracy said.

"Not anymore." Eric slowed down enough to take it all in. The collapsed porches, the broken windows, the sunken buildings. About half of the buildings were still somewhat intact, but the rest looked as if they'd been stepped on by some careless giant.

Behind them the clomping of boots grew louder.

"Come on." Eric continued jogging down the main street, around overturned cars, rusting bicycles, parched white bones.

"Cats?" Tracy asked, staring at the bones.

"Too large."

"Dogs?"

"Still too large."

"Shit."

He guided her across the street, passed the storefronts with their glassless windows. A Bob's Big Boy restaurant was nestled between a Christian bookstore and a sporting goods store. Most of the books still rested neatly on the shelves of the bookstore, but the sporting goods store was stripped bare, the glass showcases smashed, the shelves torn down. The window facing the street of the Bob's Big Boy was also shattered, a few jagged pieces stuck in the frame. On the Formica table just inside the window was a scattering of bones. One was obviously a human skull.

"Definitely not puma," Tracy said.

Eric dragged her along the sidewalks, jumping over debris, overturned newspaper stands, abandoned furniture that had been thrown off cars and trucks as people scrambled to escape with whatever they could, not yet realizing that the whole state was cut off from the rest of the world.

"In here," he said, shouldering open the stubborn door to the Presidential Hotel. The lobby was small. A plain wooden counter with cubicles for room keys and messages dominated half the room. The other half had a gift shop, but whatever gifts had once been in there were gone. The back of the lobby had a large, ornate stairway that lead to the rooms upstairs.

"All right, you dinks," Dobbs barked at his men as they entered the town. "No need trying to be subtle about this. They know we're here and we know they're here. So we track 'em down, box 'em in, and then, and only then, we blow their fuckin' heads into stuffed cabbage. OK?"

"Upstairs," Eric whispered.

Tracy nodded.

They climbed the staircase carefully, unsure of its strength, especially after seeing so many collapsed buildings. But it seemed solid enough as they captured each step, easing their weight forward, waiting for their foot to crash through the wood and give them away.

The doors were all closed upstairs. A couple of

rats darted between their legs, running for safety at the other end of the hall.

Eric pulled Tracy close. "They'll search this place sooner or later. But at least from here we have the high ground and some cover. With some luck and in this dark, we might be able to take them. Or at least enough of them to make the others reconsider."

"Take them? You don't really believe that, do you?"

"Yes," he said.

She shrugged. "I like my lies better."

Eric pushed open the door. The room was even darker than the outside. But his night vision was excellent and he made his way across the room to the window without stepping on anything. Tracy held onto the crossbow slung over his shoulder, following his steps.

"Christ," she said, shuddering. "Look."

Huddled in the corner was a nest of rats, fat as opposums. There were at least four of them, but bunched together like that in the dark, it was hard to tell. They didn't bother to run, just twitched their noses at the intruders and continued burrowing in the corners.

"Don't worry about them," Eric said. "It's the rats outside we got to keep an eye on." He unslung the crossbow from his back and rested it against the wall. He drew the Walther P.38 from his waistband.

"I never saw so many goddamn bones," one of the men outside said. "Piles of 'em everywhere."

"What're you, a fuckin' archaeologist?" Dobbs

said. "You wanna study bones, let's catch Ravensmith and his bitch first. Then you can jump her bones."

A few of them laughed.

Dobbs stood in the middle of the street, leaning against an overturned Toyota. He was pretending to rest, but Eric could see his eyes sweeping the stores, searching. Even if he saw Eric he probably wouldn't tip. He'd just keep standing there, leaning, probably yawn. Then in a couple of minutes he'd gather them up and tell them real loud to move on to the next street. Within five minutes the place he'd spotted Eric would be nothing but dust and rubble. Yeah, Eric decided, Dobbs knew what he was doing.

Across the street was an empty lot. The huge banner stretched across the whole lot, attached to a small white trailer on cinder blocks. The sign read: SANTA CARLOTTA'S CAR LOT. LOTTA CARS, LOTTA DEALS, LOTTA FINANCING. 12.9%. NOT USED, JUST EX-PERIENCED.

A couple of Dobbs's men stood there scratching their heads. Eric gauged the distance. The window had no glass, so that was no obstacle. He waved Tracy away from the window, pivoting away himself. He checked his bow, made sure the bolt was snug against the string, took a deep breath, hinged around in front of the window long enough to fire the arrow, then swung to the other side next to Tracy.

"Unngh." The grunt was loud enough to carry across the street.

The man standing next to Eric's target began to shout. "Shit! Shit, man. He got Hiller. Hiller's fucking down."

Eric peeked around the edge of the window, saw Dobbs drop to the ground and wedge his body close to the Toyota, his M-16 pointing at no place in particular. "Drew?"

"Yeah?"

"What's Hiller's status?"

"His status? Dead, man. That's his status. A fucking arrow in his chest."

"Where'd it come from?"

"I dunno. We were just standing there, figuring where to look next. Then, zing, Hiller's trying to yank this arrow outta his chest. Jesus."

"That leaves five," Eric told Tracy.

"Right. And two of us."

"Hey, Drew?" Dobbs again.

"Yeah?"

"The arrow. How'd it go into his chest?"

"How? Through his heart, that's how."

"No, you dink, I mean the angle. What kinda angle? Up, down, sideways?"

"I dunno."

"Check."

Silence.

Eric cocked the bow and slid in another bolt. He aimed at Drew who was crawling out from under the trailer, bellying along the twelve yards of gravel between his cover and his dead buddy. He fired.

The bolt sank into Drew's back between the shoulder blades. He could see Drew squirming as

36

he tried to reach behind his back to pluck the arrow free. He died trying.

Suddenly the window sill exploded in a clamor of splinters and dust.

"Up there!" Dobbs shouted, firing another blast of bullets through the window.

The rats shrieked out a protest, but didn't move. However it came out, they'd eat well.

"Oops," Tracy said.

Eric shrugged. "It was a matter of time before they figured out where we were. At least now there's only four left."

"Four of them. Two of us. One window." Tracy checked her Colt Magnum. "What's the plan, General?"

"We wait. No point in trying to sneak out. At least from up here they've got to come to us."

"They could always wait for reinforcements."

"They could. But they won't. They aren't that smart."

"Not smart like us. Trapped in a hotel with a family of rats." She looked over at the rats. "Boy, are we laughing, huh, fellas?"

Eric cocked his bow, wedged a bolt along the brass runner. Placed it on the floor. He held his Walther P.38 in a two-fisted grip next to his cheek, jumped in front of the window, and squeezed off a round aimed at the base of the Toyota where Dobbs had been snuggled. He knew Dobbs wasn't there anymore, but he had to find out just where they were.

As soon as he fired, he dove to the side, just barely glimpsing the flashes as four guns fired simultaneously. The window frame was pulverized from four different angles.

"Well," Tracy said, "did you kill that damned Toyota?"

"It won't bother us again."

"Whew." He felt her body pressed up behind his as they hugged the wall. She was trembling, but fighting it. She'd been through worse before. But from the beginning she'd been tough about it. Sure, he'd been tough too, but she'd gone him one better. She'd gotten tough without losing her compassion. That was something he couldn't always claim about himself.

The gun flashes had identified where they were but not where they'd stay. By now they had probably shifted to new locations. So should he and Tracy.

"Come on. Let's try another room."

"Yeah, maybe they've got one with Magic Fingers in the bed."

"Sure. Got any quarters?"

They were duck-walking along the floor when they heard the heavy thud on the floor.

Eric saw it immediately. Apple green. RGD-5 in Cyrillic written on the side. Inside were 110 grams of TNT hooked to a percussion fuse with a delay of 3.2 to 4.2 seconds. How much of that precious time had already elapsed?

It was less than a second from the time the grenade came through the window and bounced on the floor to when Eric had bumped Tracy through the open door into the hall. Tracy shoved open the door opposite their room and continued on through. It was only as she took her first step that she realized there was no floor beneath her feet. She was falling. She grabbed for Eric, caught him off balance, and pulled him through too.

They barely felt the explosion as they dropped through the darkness.

3.

Col. Dirk Fallows sat next to the campfire, poking at the burning logs with his knife. The same knife he'd used to carve that scar along Eric Ravensmith's jaw and neck while they were both in Vietnam. On his lap sat the Walther P.38 his men had brought back, the one they claimed belonged to Eric.

"Quiz time, kid."

Timmy Ravensmith, thirteen, sat on the ground within arm's reach of Fallows. Always within arm's reach.

"You hear me, kid?"

Timmy nodded, rolled up his left shirt sleeve, exposing bruised and scabbed skin.

"Yccch," Fallows said. "Starting to look nasty. Better use the other arm."

Timmy brushed down the left sleeve, rolled up the right one. He shifted so the arm was within reach of Fallows. There were fewer bruises and scabs, but not by much.

"OK. Let's see, we'll start with the easy ones first. What kind of gun is this?"

Timmy looked up at it with dull, lifeless eyes. "Walther."

"Walther what?"

"P.38."

Col. Dirk Fallows grinned. "Very good." He patted the holstered gun riding his hip. "Just like mine. Your daddy has good taste in guns. *Had* good taste."

Timmy didn't respond. His flat eyes stared into the fire.

Dobbs stood behind Fallows and scratched his head. Christ, this was weird. He'd brought back Ravensmith's gun with the blood all over it. Now Fallows was sitting at the fire, watching the sun light up the edges of the Halo, about as close to sunrise as they got since the quakes. It was OK if you liked an orange and yellow sky. Personally, Dobbs didn't. He liked blue, with white clouds and a yellow sun. When he was a kid those were the three colors of crayon he always ran out of first. Then his folks would have to buy him a whole new set of Crayolas. Not that he liked drawing all that much. Mostly he liked the smell of the crayons, a little sweet. Later he took up

41

assembling plastic models of battleships. He didn't like models any more than he liked drawing, but he liked sniffing the glue, and battleships took the longest to assemble. Glue led to other stuff. Pills. Dust. A little burglary, dropping out of school, joining the marines. And the surprise of his life: It was easier to get dope in the fucking marines than it had been in high school.

Dobbs watched Fallows, trying to figure the guy out. Sure, he was a genius, that much was certain. He kept his two dozen troops—minus a few that Ravensmith had offed—in just about everything they wanted. Food, weapons, booze, women, drugs. If they were around, Fallows not only found them, he figured a way to take them. That was the fun part. But this thing with Ravensmith's kid was, well, goddamn weird. The way he played with the kid's head. The physical abuse, then the kindness. What was the point? The kid was worthless. And now, with Ravensmith dead, he wasn't even any good as a hostage. Dobbs thought they ought to just snuff the brat, but he kept that suggestion to himself.

Col. Dirk Fallows twisted the knife into a flaming log. "Next question, Tim. What kind of cartridge does the Walther P.38 use?"

"Uh, 9mm Parabellum."

"Correct. Muzzle velocity?"

Timmy scrunched his face up in thought. "I don't know."

"Try."

"Eleven hundred feet per second."

Fallows pulled the knife out of the fire and touched it to Timmy's wrist. The skin puckered and sizzled, a wisp of smoke puffing around the blistered skin.

Timmy neither withdrew his hand nor cried out. He continued staring into the fire.

Dobbs winced, wrinkling his nose at the sour smell of burnt flesh. Jesus fucking Christ. There just was no getting used to this. He studied Fallows's face a moment. Sometimes if you stared at things long enough, they'd start to form faces. Like if you stared at clouds, or wallpaper, or linoleum floors in bathrooms. Fallows had the kind of face you might start imagining if you stared at a slate cliff long enough. The long V-shaped head with the heavy chin. The scary blue eyes, so pale they almost had no color at all. That short brushy hair, white as a toad's belly. Hell, the guy was only forty-five, not that you'd know it from that steel body of his, but that premature white hair was still kind of a shock. The mouth was thin as a model's eyebrow. Sometimes it smiled, but even then it never looked like a smile. At best a sneer. Like a lizard after it's eaten a fat grasshopper.

Fallows continued. "The exact muzzle velocity is 1135 feet per second. Hell, Eric knew all this shit. Didn't he teach his baby boy anything?"

"He took us out shooting sometimes, just so we'd know. But he didn't like guns. Didn't want them around the house."

Fallows chuckled at that. "Well, for a guy who didn't like guns, he sure as hell smoked enough guys with them. But that doesn't matter. That was then and this is now. In this world you'd better know about guns. And not just guns, all weapons. So, let's continue the lesson." He stuck the knife back into the flaming log, twisted it as if he were cooking an imaginary marshmallow. "Rate of fire?"

"Thirty-two rounds a minute."

"Length?"

"Uh, 8.6 inches."

"Weight?"

"Unloaded, 1.7 pounds. Loaded with full eight-round clip, 2.125 pounds."

"Effective range?"

"Maximum of fifty-four yards."

Fallows nodded, grinned, patted Timmy on the head. "We'll make a soldier of you yet. The kind your daddy was, only better."

Timmy remained silent.

"See that tree over there?" Fallows pointed with the Walther.

Timmy nodded.

"Well, it's about time you learned how to shoot one of these things. All my soldiers know how to shoot." He released the safety, sighted along the barrel with one eye, and squeezed the trigger. The explosion thundered. A spray of bark puffed from the tree trunk. Fallows flipped the Walther in the air, caught it by the barrel, and handed it butt-first to Timmy. "You try."

Timmy stared at it without taking it.

"Uh, Colonel?" Dobbs said nervously.

"Yes, Dobbs?"

Dobbs stared into the colorless eyes, decided not to say anything. "Nothing, sir."

"Right." Fallows turned back to Timmy, the gun still thrust toward the boy. "Go ahead, Timmy. Take it."

Slowly, Timmy reached out, his thin fingers curling around the thick handle. His face was expressionless.

"Release the safety," Fallows said. "Just like I showed you."

Dobbs backed away a step. Christ, what was Fallows doing?

"Now, all you do is point and squeeze the trigger. Squeeze, don't jerk it. Aim."

Timmy lifted the gun with his right hand, pointed it at the tree.

"Keep your hand steady. It's going to have a bite to it, so be ready."

Timmy's hand trembled slightly as he closed one eye and sighted along the barrel.

"Don't close your eye. Time comes when you'll have to use that gun, you'll need both your eyes open."

Timmy opened his left eye. His finger tightened on the trigger.

"OK, shoot."

Timmy stood still, the gun raised, his finger frozen.

"Shoot, damn it. Pull the fucking trigger."

Suddenly Timmy swung around, the Walther P.38 waist level. He pointed it at Dirk Fallows's chest.

"Shit, kid," Fallows said.

And Timmy pulled the trigger.

4.

"You alive?"

"In a manner of speaking," Tracy said.

Eric brushed some rubble from his chest, noticed for the first time it was daylight. The orange sky filtered through what was left of the Presidential Hotel and he noticed what they hadn't seen in the dark. That the hotel was only a facade now, a lobby and the front rooms. The back half of the hotel had collapsed during the quakes. Only the doors remained. He looked up and saw the door they'd run through to avoid the grenade. The explosion had knocked it off one hinge.

"Quite a drop?" Tracy said.

"Yeah." He nodded at the broken boards and cement blocks all around them. "Good thing we had something soft to land on."

"We're lucky that way."

He looked at Tracy. Pain contorted her natural beauty into a mask of agony. Dust salted her short, reddish hair. She was trying to pull her legs out from under a chunk of plaster wall, not making much progress.

"Can you move?" Eric asked.

She worked one leg free, but her left leg remained motionless. She wiped the sweat from her forehead. "Define move."

Eric climbed over the debris, ignoring the ache in his lower back and the gouge in his right calf where one of his crossbow bolts had dug out a shallow crater of flesh. He hobbled stiffly as he walked, feeling a little like an ape.

"How bad?" she asked.

He hunched over the leg without touching it. He could tell from the angle what was wrong, and that it was plenty painful.

"How bad?" she repeated.

"Broken. In at least one place."

"Well, that does it. You'll have to save yourself, Eric. Leave me here. I'll be OK. It's better this way."

He gave her a look, shrugged. "OK."

"Like hell! What a time you pick to start believing me. Now get me the hell out of here. This baby hurts."

The back of his head pounded as if someone

were continuously tapping him with a baseball bat. He touched his fingers gingerly to the area, felt the crusted blood and matted hair. Old blood, at least.

Eric kicked over a hunk of the plaster wall next to Tracy's leg and a fat rat scampered up over her broken leg before burrowing back into the debris.

"Hey, I recognized that face," Tracy said. "We were roomies together up on the second floor."

"Looks like he's shopping for breakfast."

"Forget it, pal. You're fat enough."

Eric shaded his eyes, looked up at the dangling door above them. "I'll be right back, Trace."

"Where you going?"

"Back up there to look for my Walther."

She lifted her right hand, the skin scraped off and bleeding from the fall, but her S&W .357 still intact. "Wanna borrow mine?"

"You'd better hold onto it. Just in case."

He limped over the piles of splintered wood, dusty plaster and chunks of cement, balancing carefully on the shifting rubble. By the time he reached the front door of the hotel, his limp was almost gone and the dull throbbing at the back of his skull was only a slight pecking, like a crow nipping at his head.

He climbed the stairs to the second floor and stepped into the hallway. The dust aroused by the explosion still hung in the orange light like snow frozen in midfall. He cupped one hand over his nose and breathed shallowly as he walked down the hallway.

The room they'd been in no longer had a door. In fact, the doorway was twice what it had been. And a three-foot hole in the floor testified to where the grenade had been when it had exploded. Eric stepped over the hole and entered the room.

The narrow single bed had been pulverized, with bits of it scattered all over the room. The walls, oddly, were smeared with splotches of blood. A streak here, a blob there. But whose?

Eric searched the room carefully for his Walther and his crossbow. He found neither.

However, he did find bits and pieces of bloody fur that explained the bloody pattern on the walls. The rats. The ones that had been huddled in the corner had been splattered around the room. That's why Dobbs and the others hadn't hunted more closely for the bodies. In the dark they assumed the blood belonged to Eric and Tracy. So they'd gathered Eric's weapons and taken them back as proof for Fallows.

Eric hopped over the hole in the floor on his way out of the room, glanced down, and stopped on the other side. He knelt down, peered through the hole to the lobby below. The room was directly above the front desk. And there, lying on its back behind the desk, was his black crossbow. He scrambled down the stairs, recovered it, checked it over for breakage, found none. He cocked it and slipped a bolt next to the string. Immediately he felt a little better.

"Well," Tracy said, nodding at the bow when

he returned.

"Yeah. They got the Walther, though."

"But why didn't they get us?"

He explained his theory.

"Makes sense. Besides, after seeing what happened to their buddies, they were probably eager to accept the explanation rather than go poking through the dark for us."

"Still, it's a little deflating to think they mistook a bunch of dead rats for us."

She laughed and the movement immediately caused a sharp pain in her leg. "Owww. Damn it, Eric, don't make me laugh."

He unstrapped the canvas knapsack from her back and slung it over his arm. "We'd better get you someplace out of the sun so I can tend to your leg."

"What's your early diagnosis, doc?"

"Well, the main concern is the fracture of the femur."

"Don't dazzle me with footwork, just tell me how long it will hurt."

"Depends. A fracture is a clean break of the bone. The jagged edges of the bone contain a rich supply of nerves and when they rub against each other or any other tissue, it hurts."

"No kidding."

"The pain and swelling could continue for weeks, even months. We've got to be careful that the sharp edges of the bone don't cut a nerve or a blood vessel."

"How long, Eric?"

"One to six months."

"Christ!"

"I'll splint and tape it, that'll help."

"But one to six months! There's no way you can track Fallows with me along."

Eric sat down on a block of cement. "I can always pick up his trail again. He's not exactly keeping a low profile."

"Yeah, but there's no telling what could happen to Timmy in that amount of time."

Eric thought back on the Timmy he'd seen walking across Fallows's camp. The slight swagger, the hint of a sneer. The ice water that had washed through Eric's stomach as he recognized Fallows in Timmy's behavior. The horror.

"What are we going to do, Eric?"

He shrugged, stood up. "Get you out of the sun."

He lifted her carefully to her one good leg, wrapping her arm around his neck and half-carrying her on his hip. They made it around the corner of the building and were heading toward Bob's Big Boy when something caught Eric's eye. He squinted over at where the two men he'd killed last night were. Something was wrong.

"How long you say we were unconscious back there?"

She studied her watch. "Maybe four hours."

"Yeah. Wait here," he said, starting to uncurl her arm.

She clung tighter. "I'm getting used to hopping. Besides, I'd rather not be left alone again. Even to cross the street."

He saw that she was serious. "OK."

They hobbled across the street toward Santa Carlotta's Car Lot like clumsy partners in a three-legged race.

As they got closer, Tracy's mouth opened with shock. "Oh God!"

The two men laid about five feet apart. The guns and equipment had been stripped. That would've been Dobbs. But the other thing, Christ, who knows?

Eric lowered Tracy to the ground at least ten feet from the bodies. She was silent, keeping her mouth closed to preserve whatever food was in her stomach. She cupped both hands over her mouth and nose as if she feared the air might be contaminated.

Eric knelt next to the first man. He was about twenty-eight, with a wispy blond beard. He was naked, the same as his partner. Even the bolts that had killed them were gone. Dobbs wouldn't have wasted time stripping them. Nor would he or his men have done the other thing. The mutilation.

The first man's right hand was missing from his wrist. Scattered in the dust a few feet away were the bare bones of his fingers. One of his buttocks was missing, flesh torn in large hunks all the way down to the thigh. A few feet away his partner lay with only one leg and one arm, the clean white bones of each in a neat pile next to the trailer.

"What kind of an animal?" Tracy began.

Eric shook his head. "No animal. The hand was

severed clean here. The leg and arm on the other guy were hacked and twisted free."

"Christ, Eric. You're talking about goddamn cannibals."

"Uh-huh."

They gripped their weapons tighter and glanced around.

5.

Col. Dirk Fallows laughed.

Timmy kept the Walther P.38 thrust toward Fallows's chest and squeezed the trigger again. The hammer snapped, metal striking metal. No explosion. No bullet. Just the big, craggy face of Fallows laughing at him. He kept pulling the trigger, eight or ten times. Click, click, click . . .

Dobbs took a deep breath, not even realizing he'd stopped breathing the moment Fallows had given the kid the gun. His throat was dry from not swallowing. There were little crescents of blood on his palm from where his fingernails had dug in when he'd clenched his fist. He stared at his open hand. Shit, when had he done that? He wiped the blood on his pants. He could sure use a cigarette.

"Well, well," Fallows said, still chuckling as he

stepped toward Timmy.

Timmy winced. He lifted the gun by the barrel as if it were a hammer, but Fallows snatched it away from him.

"Hell, I'm not going to punish you, Tim. It took guts to do what you just did. The kind of guts we need around here. I'm proud of you."

Then Fallows did something that shocked Dobbs. He grabbed the kid by the shoulder and hugged him close, patting his back like an old buddy. Like a son. Christ, Dobbs thought, now I've seen everything.

Timmy didn't resist. He just stood there, zombielike, tears leaking from both eyes, feeling not good for anything. He hadn't been able to protect his sister when they'd killed her. He hadn't been able to protect his mother when they'd killed her. Now he hadn't even been able to kill the man responsible for his father's death. What good was he?

"You're going to make a first-rate soldier yet, Tim. I guarantee it. When I'm done with you, well, you'll be able to take care of yourself. And anybody you care about."

Timmy looked up. Take care of people he cared about. Yeah, wouldn't that be something.

Fallows watched Timmy's eyes and continued. "The biggest obstacle to getting to the top is fighting your way through the crowd at the bottom. Remember that, kid. And that once you get to the top, all those clowns jerking around down there are going to try to take away what's yours. You've got to know how to control them.

Use them. Or, if you have to, destroy them."

"That doesn't sound . . . right," Timmy said.

"Doesn't it? Why? Because your dad said so? Well, he didn't bother teaching you kids even part of what he knew about surviving. Look where it got you. If he was so damn right, how come you're here? How come your mother and sister aren't? What'd he do about it? Huh, what?"

Timmy shook his head furiously. "*You* killed them, not him. It was you!"

"I did what was necessary to protect myself and my people. If your father had listened to me, your mother and sister would still be alive. Think about that."

Dobbs pulled a pack of Winstons out of his pocket, shook one loose, and clamped his lips on the filter. He didn't understand Fallows's game, but whatever it was, this kid was starting to crumble. Dobbs grinned as he touched the match flame to the cigarette. Shit, that Fallows could sure mess up your mind.

"Just think about it, Tim," he said, hugging Timmy's shoulder again. "And while you're at it, think about that bitch he's been traveling with, humping every night."

"No," Timmy said, "Tracy's a friend. Mom's friend, too."

"Yeah, well, she's an even better friend to your dad. Your mom was hardly even cold before he started screwing her brains out. I wouldn't be surprised if they'd had something going even before your mom died—"

"No!"

"Maybe even before the quakes. Maybe ole Eric wasn't in all that much of a hurry to find you and your mom after all. Maybe he liked the way things worked out. Him free to take up with that Tracy woman."

Timmy fought the tears, standing stiff and upright as if he were at attention. But his shoulders shook, the tears tumbling down his cheeks like tiny boulders.

"The thing is, kid, you've got to be flexible in this world. Make new alliances." He released the empty clip from the Walther and tossed it on the ground. Then he took a full clip from his pocket and palmed it into the gun. "First thing you've got to do is trust no one. No one. Check everything yourself." He snapped a round into the chamber and thumbed off the safety. "Like I said, check everything yourself. Now you know this gun is loaded, because you saw the bullets in the clip."

Dobbs took a drag on the Winston, let the smoke curl out of his nose just for a change. What the fuck's he doing with that gun? Whatever it was, Dobbs didn't like it. "Maybe I should go check out the food supply, Colonel?"

"Yeah, OK. Only wait a second. I want you to see this."

Dobbs shrugged, puffed out a couple smoky hoops.

"What I mean, Tim, is that you have to know who can do you any good. Can get you what you want. Think about that for a moment. What is it you want right now? Don't have to tell me, just think about it. Then ask yourself this: Who is most likely going to be able to help me get it? See what I mean?"

Timmy didn't say anything, but Fallows watched the eyes, knew the kid was thinking.

"Take me, for instance. I have to trust people all the time. I send them out on a job, and I have to trust them to do it. And do it right. Well, like Dobbs here."

Dobbs straightened a little at the mention of his name. He didn't want to be involved in Fallows's weird shit.

"I send my man Dobbs out after your dad and he brings me back a fucking gun. I ask for him alive or at least the head and what do I get? A goddamn gun with some smeared blood. Could be anybody's blood, even Dobbs's for all I know."

Dobbs shifted uncomfortably, coughing a little when the smoke went down the wrong tube. He didn't like the way this was going. Something kinky here.

"Maybe your dad is dead. But maybe he's only wounded. Maybe he's looking at us right now, that big, ugly crossbow of his aimed at Dobbs's head."

Dobbs knew Fallows was playing with his mind now, but he couldn't help but look over his shoulder, take a sweep of the woods. Didn't see anything. "Christ, Colonel . . ."

Fallows ignored him. "My point, Tim, is that when you ask for something and it isn't done, then that person has not only risked your life, but the lives of everyone you're responsible for. I'm responsible for a lot of lives here. All these men you see count on me. I take that seriously. Just like I take protecting you seriously. Nothing's happened to you since you've been with me, has it?"

Timmy shrugged, rubbing his bruised and burned arm.

"That doesn't count, kid. That's lessons. I'm talking about your life. Survival. Your dad protected his family and look what happened to them. That won't happen with my little family. I won't let it." He offered the gun butt to Timmy. "But a family needs to be able to trust each other. And when that trust is broken, they need to be punished. You follow me?"

"I-I don't know." Timmy stared at the gun without taking it. Fallows spoke so quickly, and Timmy was so exhausted, it was hard to follow what was being said. It sounded right, but . . .

"Take it, Tim. Take the gun."

Dobbs flicked the cigarette into the dirt. "C'mon, Colonel, this is getting weird."

"Just bear with me a minute, Dobbs. You'll see what I'm getting at." Fallows winked at him when Timmy couldn't see.

Dobbs nodded and grinned to show he understood. He felt a little better now.

"Go on, take it." Fallows smiled, his arm still resting on Timmy's shoulder.

Slowly, Timmy reached for the gun. He hefted it, looked it over, as if checking to see if it was the same gun with the bullets. Or had Fallows made a switch?

"There's the safety. Check it first. That's right. Now it's off. Guess all we need now's a target." He looked around, his hand still firmly gripping Timmy's shoulder. "Well, I guess we'll just have to use ole Dobbs there." He chuckled.

Dobbs chuckled too, but it came out more like a choke. And his skin had paled considerably.

"Go on, Tim." Fallows's voice began to take on a lulling rhythm, yet with a harsh edge, a commanding tone. "There's the man who may have killed your father. Who at least tried to. Look at the blood on the handle. That could be your daddy's blood. Pumping out of a hole in his chest while he was dying. Go ahead, pull the trigger."

Dobbs looked confused, but didn't move. He stood there frozen like a cat caught in a car's headlights.

Fallows continued, squeezing Timmy's shoulder as he kneeled beside the boy. "But I say he probably didn't kill your daddy. That Eric Ravensmith is probably alive right now, out there with some woman who surely is not your mother. And if he is alive, then Dobbs here has put the rest of us in jeopardy. He has risked all our lives by not doing his job properly. You and I, Tim, we have a responsibility to protect these men, just like your daddy should have protected you and your mother and sister. We won't fail like he did, will we? Will we?"

Timmy shook his head. "No."

"Then shoot. Shoot the bastard."

Timmy lifted the gun.

61

"Fuck, Colonel," Dobbs said. "He's gonna do it."

"Shoot, Tim. Squeeze that trigger. We have to protect our family. *Squeeze the goddamned trigger!*"

Timmy pointed the gun at Dobbs's chest, his hand quivering as his finger hooked around the trigger.

"Shoot!" Fallows screamed. But when Timmy didn't, Fallows reached over and clamped his huge hand around Timmy's, his finger pressing Timmy's small finger against the trigger until the explosion.

The gun jerked back at the same time Dobbs jerked back, the front of his chest opening like a red orchid suddenly in bloom. He flopped to the ground, his right foot kicking a pattern in the dirt while his leg spasmed. But he was already dead.

Fallows unpeeled Timmy's cold fingers from the gun and patted him on the back. "Congratulations, son." He grinned. "You just killed a man for *not* killing your father."

6.

Tracy looked out through the broken window of Bob's Big Boy and watched him running across the street. She laid her .357 back on her lap, folded her book face-down on the Formica table, and smiled. "Well now, what do we have here? A wandering minstrel?"

"Nobody here but us rock 'n' rollers," Eric said, standing outside the window. He held up the battered Martin guitar by the neck.

"You play that thing?"

"A little. Long time ago."

"I didn't know that. All this time and I didn't know you played the guitar."

He shifted the crossbow out of the way and strummed a C chord. "Everyone at the party laughed when I sat down to play." He strummed a

D chord. "But thanks to Jiffy guitar lessons, now I'm asked to play at all the parties. Amaze your friends and confound your enemies." He strummed a few chord combinations that sounded like Elvis Presley's "Heartbreak Hotel."

Tracy applauded, laughing. "Where'd you find it?"

"The Exxon station down the road. In the john. I think someone was sitting in there when the quake hit and ran off without it. Funny thing is, someone had gone in there afterward and broken open the toilet paper dispenser. Took all the toilet paper, but left this guitar."

"Priorities change."

"Yeah, I know. Still . . ." He shrugged.

She held up her tattered paperback novel. "Found this under one of the tables back there. Along with a used diaper, a pair of high heels, a bill for chicken snack and a strawberry milk shake, and a Bob's menu."

"Lucky you. Finally something new to read."

"I read the menu three times all the way through, kind of forcing myself to hold off on the book."

"What about the religious bookstore next door?"

"C'mon, Eric, you know me. I don't want to read about someone worse off then we are. I want escape. Christ, it's like a romantic thing, almost sexual, not wanting to rush right in and read it. Prolonging it. Right away I told myself I was only going to read five pages a day, make it last. I'm already fifty pages into it." She adjusted her

64

bandaged leg, wincing. "Thing about all this survival stuff is, it gets pretty boring."

Eric laughed. "You didn't think that a few hours ago when we were being chased or even an hour ago when we discovered what Bob's Big Boy's been serving lately."

"Yeah, well, you know what I mean. OK, we spend a lot of time just trying to stay alive, find water and food and keep from being turned into a blue-plate special. But after a while, your mind kind of adjusts to danger and accepts that as normal. Almost routine. You know?"

"I know. Like in the army. Even in combat there were times we'd rather have faced enemy bullets than sit around and wait another minute. That is, until the bullets actually started flying." He looked at the book cover and smiled. *Missionary Stew* by Ross Thomas. "Unfortunate title, considering."

"That's one thing that isn't so boring. Those men chewed down to the bone." She shuddered. "What do you think that means, Eric?"

Eric climbed through the gaping window and slid into the booth across the table from Tracy. She had her leg propped up on a chair, the bandages made from some *E.T.* sheets he'd found in one of the homes. The wood splints were cut from pine panelling he'd ripped from the walls of someone's den. He'd done a pretty good job, considering their resources, and was thinking that maybe the leg wasn't as bad as he'd first thought. At least Tracy didn't seem to be in as much pain.

"Not a lot of things it could mean. Somebody's

hungry and eating the bodies. Not all that unusual when you think about it. In a way, it even makes sense."

"Jesus, Eric."

"I mean it. We've got a definite food shortage considering how many people are not prepared to hunt or grow their own. It would figure they'd turn to cannibalism. Kind of natural, in a way."

"Look, you've known me long enough to know I'm not that squeamish anymore. I've seen about every atrocity possible since the quakes. But this." She shook her head. "This is too much, I don't care how natural. It's damn spooky."

"Well, cannibalism usually takes longer to occur unless there are unusual circumstances."

"You don't call being shaken free of the rest of the continent by an earthquake unusual? Or being enclosed by a dome of gas formed from biological and chemical weapons a teeny bit unusual?"

"Not for California. Come to think of it, that arm of yours is looking pretty tasty. Hmmmm."

She reached across the table and swatted him with her book. "As I recall, you've had a taste or two before."

He grinned. "You must be doing something right. I keep coming back for more."

She leaned over, her breasts pressed against the edge of the Formica table. "That's as far as I can move, pal."

Eric stood and leaned over, their lips meeting over the table that a few hours ago had been piled with human bones. They kissed slowly and warmly, tongues polishing each other.

When they finished, Tracy sat back and sighed. "Doesn't it seem to you like we're getting more than our share of physical abuse? Me breaking the same damn leg that was shot last month. It's like we belong to Wound of the Month Club or something."

"Beats dead."

"It sure helps to have a deep thinker like you around."

He laid the crossbow on the table, fit the guitar on his lap, strummed a few quiet chords.

"You think they're still out there?" Tracy asked.

"Who? Fallows?"

"No, the guys with the bad munchies. You think they're still hanging around?"

"Probably. It's only been a couple of hours since they dined on those two guys."

"I got this picture of a gang of them watching us right now, one of them with a pad and pencil taking orders. I'll take a thigh. Save the wishbone for me. Do humans have wishbones?"

"Do chickens have funny bones?"

"Christ, Eric. Give me a break. I'm talking about being turned into a boxed lunch and you're sitting there acting like early Bob Dylan."

"Relax. The fact that they didn't totally consume the bodies means that we probably scared them off. So, chances are they're not very heavily armed."

Tracy hefted her S&W .357 Combat Magnum. "First one to show me a sharp tooth is going to be swallowing lead."

"Swallowing lead?"

She shrugged. "I've been saving that phrase all my life."

Eric's fingers began plucking a soft melody on the guitar. He stopped, tuned it, plucked, tuned it again. When he played again, Tracy noticed his face growing pale, his mouth pulled into a tight grimace. He stared at the strings as he played, but not at the strings exactly, rather, at the dark hole in the middle of the sounding board. It was as if he saw something inside that hole, a portal to some time past. She sat and watched him, knowing he probably wasn't even aware that he was humming along.

She studied his face, the skin tanner now, more wrinkles around the eyes than his age would call for. They had been recent additions, the result of living outdoors. Facing the sun and rain daily. She knew what all this nature had done to her face, so she only looked in her compact mirror once in the morning when she was combing her hair. That was enough. The toughening of the skin into some human leather, the hands and feet thick with calluses, their bodies hard with taut muscles seemed to reflect an inner process too. A hardening of their emotions, callousing of their humanity. Yet somehow each acted as some kind of lotion for each other, soothing, moistening each other's heart. At least it had worked so far.

"That Paul Simon?" she asked.

Eric smiled. "'St. Judy's Comet.' I used to sing it to Timmy and Jennifer. Like a lullaby. They used to pretend to fall asleep just to make me feel good, like they felt sorry for the old guy sitting there with his guitar and corny song. The moment

I left the room they'd start throwing pillows at each other. You know, it meant more to me that they tried to fake it than if I'd really put them to sleep. Understand?"

Tracy nodded. Talking about Annie or the kids was unusual for them. Kind of an understood no man's land. Eric had done his best to bury these memories, as if some inner earthquake had destroyed them. It was the only way he could live with what had happened. And with his mission to rescue Timmy from Dirk Fallows.

"Won't be able to call him Timmy anymore," Eric said. "He's grown. An inch, maybe more. Better start thinking of him as Tim now, or Timothy. No more Timmy." He slid his left hand along the frets of the guitar, finger picking and staring into the dark hole in the guitar. When he started to sing, Tracy realized for the first time that she had never heard him sing since that last night at University Camp. When Jenny and Annie had been murdered. The kids had given him a beat-up old cassette player with a tape of the Beatles' old songs. He'd sung along with them that night, but never again. Until now.

He sang softly, almost to himself, in a voice that was pleasant but not very good. Still, it made Tracy want to hug him, bury her face in his chest and keep hugging him for hours. Singing. She hadn't realized how much she'd missed it until now. She joined in.

Little sleepy boy
Do you know what time it is?
Well the hour of your bedtime's

Long been past
And though I know you're fighting it
I can tell when you rub your eyes
You're fading fast
Fading fast.

As they sang, Eric glanced out into the street and saw the sky suddenly filled with drifting paper. He recognized the familiar yellow paper of the government's bulletins, dropped on the first day of every month. It was the only way the survivors knew what was going on outside the island of California. It was also the only way most could keep the months separate. But something was wrong here. This wasn't the usual drop.

Eric slid the guitar onto the table and grabbed his crossbow. "Didn't they just drop these two weeks ago?"

"Uh-huh. Two weeks yesterday."

"I don't like it."

"What's not to like, aside from the litter problem? So they've decided to increase the frequency of distribution. Great. I wonder what Farrah's done with her hair now."

"It's not that simple. The government doesn't change routine unless something special's up." He stood on the seat and climbed out through the window. Once outside he scooped up a couple of the single-sheet flyers and climbed back through the window. He handed one to Tracy. They both read silently.

"Christ!" she said, balling it up and throwing it out the window. "Evacuate! To where?"

70

Eric read the paper again. Then again. His eyes narrowed and he chewed on his lower lip.

"What?" Tracy said.

He looked up. "Huh?"

"What're you thinking? I recognize that hunched expression. Something's going on."

"This," he said, tapping the paper. "They tell us to evacuate the whole area within a fifty-mile radius of Santa Barbara because they plan to conduct special experiments on the Long Beach Halo."

"Santa Barbara's only about twenty miles from here."

Eric ignored her. "They claim that the experiments will involve dangerous chemicals and radiation that can kill us, cause cancer, and give us bad breath."

"So? We've got a week to clear out. Even a gimp like me can make it out of here by then. Tell you the truth, I'm not so crazy about the local cuisine anyway. Eric?"

Eric crushed the paper in his fist. He was nodding to himself as he paced next to the table. His face was smooth, untroubled, as if he'd just made an important decision. There was a hint of a smile on his face. Suddenly he picked up the guitar and smashed it against a nearby table.

"Eric, you're starting to scare me," Tracy said.

"Let's pack up," he said. "We're going."

"Great, where? San Francisco? Fresno? Los Angeles?"

He flattened the yellow sheet on the table. At the bottom was a map of the island of California with a big red X where the experiments were scheduled to take place and concentric circles extending for fifty miles in every direction. The kill zone. Eric put his finger on the big red X and smiled. "This is where we're going. Santa Barbara."

Book Two:

THE REGION OF SORROW

Better to reign in hell than serve in heav'n.
—Milton

7.

Paige Lyons rolled over in her bed and nudged the guy snoring next to her. "Hey, Steve. We're on TV."

Steve didn't budge.

She shook his naked shoulder, not pausing as she usually did to appreciate his sculpted muscles. "Steve. Wake up time, Captain."

Steve shrugged her hand from his shoulder and kept snoring.

"Shit." She sat up and looked at the blue digital clock set in the Hitachi VCR next to the TV. 2:30 a.m. She slid over to the edge of the bed, liking the way the satin sheets felt against her naked backside, and reached over for the remote control box on the bedstand. She knocked over an empty wine glass that bounced on the thick carpeting without breaking. The sudden movement frightened her black cat who'd been curled under the bed. The cat ran out of the room and down the stairs.

Paige Lyons stabbed the Mute button and the sound came back on the TV. The newscaster was Cindy Treetown, an ex-classmate of Paige's from Bennington. They'd once double-dated to a Crosby, Stills & Nash concert with a couple of Yalies who'd tried to get them stoned on grass that turned out to be mostly oregano. The Yalies were both MBA candidates more angry at having made a bad business deal than the fact that their dates had been in the restroom for forty-five minutes. When the Yalies finally tumbled that something was wrong, Paige and Cindy had already sneaked out through the crowd with two Penn State guys they'd met near the restrooms. They'd both come a long way since then, Cindy had pointed out yesterday right before she'd interviewed Paige for the cable news channel.

". . . About the space shuttle *Columbia*'s mission, Cindy was saying, her face set in the typical newscaster's stony expression. "When interviewed yesterday, astronaut Paige Lyons insisted it was just a routine flight."

The screen filled with Paige's face. A hint of makeup, the long, blond hair parted down the middle, curving softly around her face "like the disheveled wings of a mischievous angel," Norman Mailer had described it for *Life*. A funny little man, she remembered, who over lunch told her there was one principle that guided his whole

76

professional life. Alimony.

"Informed sources tell us that this mission was thrown together rather quickly, Dr. Lyons," Cindy was asking.

"That's somewhat true, Cindy," Paige said. "Part of the purpose of this mission is to see how flight-alert we are in case of a space emergency. How quickly can we activate a shuttle and be in space to affect repairs to a space station or a malfunctioning satellite? That's what we want to find out."

Paige smiled at her image on the screen. "What a good little liar you are, dear."

"So it's strictly routine," Cindy asked. "Including using the old *Columbia*?"

"The taxpayers bought it, they might as well get their money's worth, don't you think?"

"What about rumors that you intend to focus special attention on the California situation?"

"Sure, we intend to observe it, study it. We want to make sure the so-called Long Beach Halo isn't shifting and starting to move toward the continent. But that's all. Just observation for now."

Paige shook her finger at the screen. "If Sister Theresa could see your fibbing little butt now. Christ."

". . . All wish you good luck."

Paige clicked the Mute button again. The best part was over. The lying.

She flicked the Play button to start the VCR. A bunch of the guys at NASA had given her this tape as a good luck gift. A blue movie called

77

Insatiable starring Marilyn Chambers. She had started watching it alone that afternoon. Steve had already called twice, as he did every day, begging to come over. She'd refused. She was halfway through the movie when he'd called again. This time she'd said OK. Just for a while.

Now she couldn't get rid of him.

She looked around her dark Washington, D.C. bedroom. She studied it in the light of the flickering TV while Marilyn Chambers romped in the pool with another naked woman. The room, like the entire two-bedroom condominium, was perfect. It had taken her years to get everything just right, the wallpaper, the paintings, the furniture. Every detail was carefully planned, from the shape and color of the soap bars to the type of plants. Not a speck of dust or slipper out of place. The place was like her life. In perfect order.

The cat slinked back in, sniffed the wine glass by the bed, pawed at it. Paige leaned over the bed and snagged the glass, setting it back on the nightstand.

No, it was more than orderly. It was luxurious. Satin sheets, down bedding, solid brass bathroom fixtures, skylight over the extra-large tub. Now *that* was the right stuff.

The only thing out of place was Naval Capt. Steve Connors, also scheduled for the *Columbia*'s flight in two days. She looked at him and frowned. He was like a dirty dish or a full ash tray. He threw off the whole balance of the decor. She wished she could somehow vacuum him away.

She shook him roughly. "C'mon, Steve. Time to haul ass."

He stirred, opened one groggy eye. Christ, now he was smacking his lips. "Huh?"

"Get up, get dressed."

"Huh?" He sat up, scratched his head.

Paige shook her head. He'll scratch his crotch next, I swear. "You've got to go."

He scratched his crotch.

"I knew it," she said.

"Knew what? What time is it?"

"Time for you to get in your little red Porsche and get back to your own pad. Don't you miss those lovely posters of Tina Turner?"

"Quit it, Paige. You know I haven't had that one for years."

"That's always been one of your problems. No loyalty." She shoved his shoulder. "Go on. Scoot."

"Gee, Paige." She saw the hurt expression on his face as he climbed out of bed, standing there naked, a man's muscular body with a little boy's emotions. She felt a little guilty.

"Sorry, Steve. But you know how the reporters are keeping a watch on us. If the gang at NASA knew we were doing this, they'd can our asses. This is just the kind of publicity they don't want."

"That the real reason?" Christ, now he was pouting.

"Yeah, sure."

He smiled. "You weren't too worried about publicity two years, three months and eighteen days ago."

Here it comes, she thought. That's just the reason she'd kept him away from her for the past six months. He always came back to the same thing. Damn. "Look, Steve, we've been through all that. It was a mistake, we both agreed."

"I've changed my mind. I liked being married to you. Even if it was a secret between just us."

"That's the point, Steve. That's why we got divorced just as quietly. You know how they feel about relationships between people in the program. They'd boot us out in a minute. It's better this way."

Most of that was the truth. NASA used to discourage personal relationships between the sexes with their astronauts, but they stopped short of condemning a marriage once it occurred. That is until Tina Rydell and Phil Stewart got married. Phil was photographed in bed with a female NASA technician and an ugly divorce ensued, played out every night on national news. The publicity damaged the whole image of the astronauts and ever since, NASA lived in fear of the same thing happening again. Resulting, as such things often do, in a budget cut. NASA would fire them both if they knew. The press would hound them for months, not to mention women's groups who'd accuse her of single-handedly setting back the women's movement by a decade. Thing is, they'd be right. Oh God, why'd she let him come over?

"When do you want to get together again?" he asked as he pulled his jogging pants over his narrow waist. "Tomorrow?"

"It is tomorrow, Steve. I think we'd better just cool it for now. What with the mission and everything."

"Yeah, maybe you're right."

That was easy.

"But afterwards," he said, zipping his jacket over his bare chest. "Then we try again, OK? Make it work this time. You drop out of the program."

"We'll see, Steve. Right now, we've got enough to think about with this mission. This is no routine flight."

"Yeah." He glanced at the TV screen, watched Marilyn Chambers hike up her white skirt and lie back on the pool table while the chauffeur unzipped his pants.

"Bye, Steve." Paige stood up and held the bedroom door open. She placed a hand on her slender hip. He looked at her, grinned. She liked the reaction she got from men when they looked at her naked body. Surprise mostly the first time. It was even better than they'd imagined it to be. Lean, yet curvy too. Muscular, yet smooth. She never needed to stand on a scale; she always knew her exact weight. "See you in a few hours at the briefing."

"Right. Later." He marched down the stairs and out the front door.

She sighed with relief when the door closed. Steve was pretty easy to handle, like most men. She had yet to meet one who was more important to her than her career. OK, she'd made a mistake a couple years ago. At a moment when she'd had some doubts and fears about her future. Marriage seemed a good idea. At least she'd been smart enough to keep it a secret.

She climbed back in bed. Her cat had taken Steve's place under the covers. Paige leaned back against the slippery satin pillows and watched Marilyn Chambers's contortions. Anything to take her mind off the mission.

"Do you understand why you're here, Dr. Lyons?"

"Of course," Paige said.

"Good." The CIA man had said his name was Plummer, but Paige had been around Washington enough not to believe any information that was offered free. Plummer was about sixty with dark black hair. Not a single gray hair. They must all be using the president's barber, she thought. "You've already gone through the special training, as has your crew, Connors, Budd, La Porte and Piedmont. You should be able to handle the assortment of weapons we've stored in the craft."

"Yes, sir. I've been shooting since I was a kid."

Plummer glanced at the open file on the desk in front of him. "Yes. I see you even won a couple NRA trophies."

"Yeah, when I was twelve and fifteen. I stopped shooting competitively after I discovered boys."

"Twelve and *fourteen*," he corrected her, tapping the file in front of him. "Ever kill a man, Dr. Lyons?"

She thought of a dirty answer and laughed. "No."

"Don't hunt."

"Nope."

"Well." He looked disappointed. He closed the folder and pushed it aside as if to display that what came next was off the record. "I know your instructors have told you this before, but let me reaffirm their teaching. Shooting a person is not the same as shooting a target. The fact that you haven't even hunted disturbs me. If it were up to me, I'd pull you from this assignment right now."

"Because I'm a woman?"

"Because the nature of your mission is such that you are guaranteed to *have to kill*. It's not just a possibility. You will have to blow some people's brains out. Some people who used to be pillars of their communities, people with children, with grandchildren. Even women. I don't think you're up to it."

"Not like Steve Connors."

"At least he's had combat experience in Vietnam."

"Yeah, flying overhead in a jet fighter. He never saw one person he killed up close."

"True. Hell, if it were up to me, the whole damn mission would be run by CIA personnel. But we don't have any trained astronauts, so we have to rely on you people. Especially you, Dr. Lyons. You're the key to the whole operation."

"I know."

"This is really a first. NASA and the CIA on a

joint venture. Could be the start of a beautiful friendship, eh?"

"I don't think that's what NASA's about, Mr. Plummer."

"Of course not. Still it can't hurt to help each other out on occasion. Remember, NASA came to us on this one."

"If I'm not mistaken, the president came to you and ordered you to help."

Plummer laughed for the first time and Paige noticed one dead tooth in the front among the gleaming white ones. "You know your politics, Dr. Lyons. But then, with your background, you would, eh?" He pulled the file folder in front of him again. "Then you won't be surprised when I tell you that if you blow it, I'll be the one who looks bad around here. You were selected for this mission because of your special, uh, knowledge. Everything hinges on you. Certainly there's plenty to inspire your best efforts, but I'm going to offer you one more bit of motivation." He lifted a sheet of paper from the file and held it up to her. "Yup, it's a photocopy of your marriage license with Captain Steve Connors."

Paige Lyons didn't say anything. They had been so careful, driving all the way up to Pennsylvania and finding some tipsy justice of the peace to perform the ceremony. They'd been dressed in running suits and hats. And at the time, they hadn't even been famous. No one knew who they were. The whole thing had taken fifteen minutes and they'd figured it would be forgotten.

"Yes, Dr. Lyons, we were keeping tabs on you

84

even then. This took some digging, especially after Captain Connors accidentally shook my men in that Maryland rainstorm, but eventually we asked enough questions to come up with this. Of course, we have a copy of the divorce, too." He held up the document and grinned.

"What do you expect me to do?"

"Your best, that's all any of us can do."

"For God's sake, Plummer, he's my father. Don't you think I'll do everything I can to get him out of there?"

"Yes, yes I do. Only getting your father out of there isn't enough. In fact, it isn't even the primary purpose of this mission. Getting those scientific papers of his out is. If he's still alive and you can get him out too, fine. If not, we still want those papers. Your father finally came up with a practical solution to the weapons in space program and we were sending agents to pick up those papers when the quake hit. Somewhere on that damn island is a packet of blueprints that will change the nature of this country's military defense. We're talking world survival here."

"So what you're saying is that finding my father is secondary to finding his papers."

"I just don't want you to waste time, Dr. Lyons. Your father may already be dead."

"Perhaps. In any event, I keep my mind on finding the papers. If I come back empty-handed, you get me thrown out of NASA. Right?"

"Blunt, but correct. The space shuttle will only be there a finite amount of time. Two days. Then it takes off with or without your father. With or without his papers. With or without you."

Paige stared coldly at the CIA man.

He smiled, that dead tooth gray among the white ones. "You know that mountain retreat of his. You know how to get there, where he might have hidden the papers, what they might look like. Your Ph.D. in physics will help there. If anybody can find him, it's you. The only problem is we don't know what else you'll find there. Our scientists figure there's no government of any kind left, except maybe small communities like medieval Europe."

"Or the street gangs of the cities."

"Yeah, even better. We just want you to know what you'll be up against."

Paige Lyons stood up, her long legs lifting her a couple of inches taller than the short CIA agent. "Don't worry, Mr. Plummer," she said with an icy smile. "You've convinced me that I'll be able to kill a human being."

8.

"Eric, come here! Cougar tracks. I swear."

"Tracy."

"Don't give me that boy-who-cried-wolf shit. I'm telling you they're cougar tracks or puma tracks or whatever the hell you want to call them. Look."

Eric brushed aside a tree branch and stepped over some bristles and soggy yellow leaflets warning residents to evacuate. They'd been hiking through the woods for five days. Santa Barbara was just on the other side of the hills and today was the day that the experiments on the Long Beach Halo were supposed to take place.

"Look at that," Tracy pointed with her crutch. "I told you, damn it."

Eric knelt next to the tracks and studied them.

"See? Okay, maybe I was kidding before about seeing one, but look. Jesus, the size of 'em."

Eric stood up, peered through the trees to a clearing. A small house stood alone at the top of a knoll. "Come on, let's check out that house. Might be empty."

"I was right, wasn't I? Cougar, right?"

"Nope."

"What do you mean? Look, damn it. The pads, the four toes, the long claw marks. Four of them here. Another four there. Like it was running."

"Very good," Eric said, meaning it. "Only it's not a cougar, not any kind of a cat. Probably a wolf or a wild dog."

"But the claws—"

"Cats don't leave claw marks, they keep them retracted. Also, there are four footprints together here. Cats leave only two."

Tracy frowned. "What're you saying? They tiptoe?"

"No, it's called directly registering. That means that when they pick up their front foot, the rear foot on the same side falls directly into the front print so it looks like a single print. Cats are the only animal family that does that. However, a fox will also directly register."

Tracy gave him a cold stare and turned away. "I hate you sometimes."

Eric smiled, stepped up behind her, slipped his arms under her crutches and wrapped them around her. "You love it when I tell you crap like that. Makes you feel outdoorsy. Admit it."

"Ha. If I felt any more outdoorsy you'd have to

mow my legs."

Eric laughed, kissed her neck. "Hmmm. I see what you mean. You could use a bath. Your neck looks like it's got cougar tracks on it."

"Me? *Me*?" She broke away from him. "You're the one who went for a midnight dip in a cesspool the other night. Christ, you smell like Pittsburgh."

He stepped closer to her, their faces only inches apart. A smile twitched at his lips. "I thought you liked Pittsburgh."

She laughed, pressed her lips against his, mashing them hard. She let her crutches fall to the ground. Immediately, she felt his powerful arms lift her onto her toes, pull her body next to his, crush it there with just the right amount of pressure. The dull ache in her broken leg seemed to stop for a moment. When she pulled her lips away from his, she was panting a little. "Do we have time for this?"

"I'll check my schedule."

"You know what I mean. Today's the big day. White man's silver birds come from sky. Drop chemicals on primitive natives down here."

Eric shrugged. "I told you, that's a crock. If the government was going to do something like that, they wouldn't pick Santa Barbara. Population density is too great. It makes more sense to try this kind of thing over the desert."

"Eric, we're talking about the government."

He laughed. "Yeah, right. Still, something is going on. There's a reason they wanted this place evacuated. Something they don't want us to see."

"And so we've got to see it."

"No. Not necessarily. But I know Colonel Dirk Fallows will. He won't believe those flyers any more than we did."

"Uh, than *you* did. I believed them."

"You're here."

She nodded at the crutches on the ground. "I wasn't given a lot of choices."

Eric stared at her for a moment. She was right. He hadn't considered her at all. He'd thought only of the opportunity to outwit Fallows. For once to know where he was going and get there first, instead of having to track him. This was his chance to rescue Tim. Nothing else had mattered.

"You're sure he's coming?" Tracy asked.

"I'm sure. He's a master at exploiting opportunity. And when the government doesn't want you someplace, that's a guaranteed opportunity begging for someone like him."

"What do you think it really is?"

"I don't know."

Tracy stooped down with awkward grace, her bandaged leg balanced straight out, and snatched up her crutches. She wedged one under each arm. "I guess the romantic mood has been broken."

They started for the house in the clearing. Eric lead the way with Tracy keeping pace remarkably well despite her crutches.

"I saw this guy with one leg run the New York Marathon on these things one year," she huffed as she swung next to Eric. "Young kid, maybe seventeen. I kept wondering what the people behind him with two legs were thinking as they tried to catch up."

"Probably that winning the race wasn't as important as being able to at least run in it."

"Uh-oh. There goes that deep thinking again. You know what Einstein said, 'I shall never believe that God plays craps with the world.'"

"He said dice. 'I shall never believe that God plays dice with the world.'"

"You're no fun. Just because you used to be a history professor doesn't mean you know everything. You can't believe everything you read in books. My uncle Gerald was a gardener for Einstein when he was at Princeton. Uncle Gerald had just told Albert that the azaleas he'd planted last season were all dead of rot. Professor Einstein was devastated. Uncle Gerald tried to cheer him up by telling him that in that particular climate, planting azaleas was a crap shoot. To which Einstein replied, 'I shall never believe that God plays craps with the world.' He later polished it up using the word dice."

Eric stopped in the middle of the field and stared at Tracy. "Is that true?"

Tracy kept swinging ahead choppily on her crutches, laughing with each hop. She glanced over her shoulder at Eric and smiled. "Gotcha."

They approached the cabin downwind. Immediately Eric knew something was wrong. "Down," he whispered. "Down."

Both of them dropped to the ground, letting the long grass surround them. Tracy had her .357 clutched in both hands. Eric checked the bolt in his crossbow.

"What?" Tracy asked, eyes raking the house for movement. "You see something?"

Eric shook his head. "Smell something."

Tracy took a deep sniff. The usual smells: burned wood from the many campfires and brush fires that swept unmolested through huge portions of the state. There was always the smell of fire in the air. But there was something else. Something rotten. "What is it?"

"Something dead. Probably human." He pushed up to one knee. "Wait here."

"Count on it."

He gave her a smile and was off, dodging in zigzags toward the modest weather-beaten house. She saw him slam up against the house, kick open the door, then crouch into the dark room, his crossbow sweeping for a target. Then he was gone.

Tracy waited, ears straining for the sound of an arrow, a gun, a knife, a muffled cry for help. Maybe she was too far away to hear. Her stomach sloshed and growled, but otherwise there was silence.

Finally, Eric appeared at the door and waved at her to come up to the house. She waved back and he disappeared back into the house.

As she climbed slowly to her feet, pulling herself up with one crutch, something odd occurred to Tracy. Eric's crossbow had been fired. As he'd waved to her with one hand, his crossbow had been gripped in his other hand, but there was no bolt in it and the string was uncocked.

Had he fired at something? Or was someone in the house? Someone holding Eric prisoner and waiting for her to come too?

Tracy hopped slowly toward the house, her gun balanced awkwardly as she held it and maneuvered the home-made crutches at the same time. What would she do? Refuse to go any further? They might kill Eric. But if she kept going, they'd probably kill both of them. With both dead there was no chance of saving Tim. At least with her alive, she could try.

But would she? With Eric gone would she try to save Tim? Probably not, she admitted.

She kept moving toward the house.

9.

They'd been watching the sky all day. Their faces were fearful, their sweaty hands clenched tightly around their weapons.

"Quit looking up," Fallows commanded. "The only thing you have to be afraid of is down here standing in front of you."

Still, the men moved slowly through the woods. Santa Barbara was a good twenty miles away. If they were going to get there in time to investigate whatever was going on, they'd have to quit dragging their asses and hurry. Fallows surveyed his men and smiled. Looks like they'd need some inspiration.

"Hey, Phelps." Fallows waved the tall ex-CHP officer over to him. "Got a cancer stick?"

"Sure, Colonel." Phelps dug into his cotton

shirt and pinched a Virginia Slim out of the pack. "This is all I got."

"That's OK. We've come a long way, baby. Right?"

"Yes, sir."

"Damn right. But then we got a long way to go. Right?"

"Yes, sir."

Fallows snatched the ancient Zippo lighter from his pocket and flamed the cigarette. The rest of the men had stopped marching to wait for Fallows. A few kept glancing up at the sky.

Tim Ravensmith stood next to Fallows. Within arm's reach. He had Eric's Walther P.38 tucked into his waistband, but there were no bullets for the gun.

"You boys have been moving a bit slower than I like. We're behind schedule." He puffed smoke from the Virginia Slim up toward the sky. Then he bent over and picked up one of the soggy yellow flyers that were littered everywhere. "I get the feeling that you fellas don't trust my judgment. That so?"

"We trust you, Colonel," someone said. A chorus of agreement followed.

"Good. That's good." Fallows put his hand on Phelps's shoulders and turned him around to face the rest of the troops. Fallows stood directly behind Phelps now. "Because you have to trust me to know the way the tiny government mind works. I have no doubt that they wouldn't hesitate to conduct experiments that would be deadly to the inhabitants. Hell, many of you were

95

in the service or worked as cops or firemen. You know what stupid things they're capable of doing."

There was murmured agreement.

"But you also know that this is not the place they'd try something like that. Nor is this"—he waved the flyer—"the way they'd go about doing it. They want something here. Or they want to do something here. I don't know what, but I know it will prove profitable for us."

They nodded support, but he could still see the fear in their eyes. Words would not be enough this time. They needed a more dramatic demonstration.

"Maybe they're dropping some kind of monitoring station. Something we can hold for ransom until they get us off this island." Fallows gently thumbed open the Zippo lighter. "We could be back on the mainland in a matter of weeks." He spoke loudly to cover the sound of his thumb flicking the flame to life. He touched the flame to the tail of Phelps's cotton shirt. It turned black at first, then a small flame ripped up the back of the shirt.

"Shit!" Phelps screamed, trying to swat at his back, thinking at first he'd been stung by some giant wasp. Then the flame was all over his back and he knew. "Help! God, help!"

Fallows booted him in the backside, sending him forward, arms windmilling to keep balance. "Now that's how I want you all to move. With speed and dedication. Like Phelps there."

Phelps spun like a flaming dervish. No one

moved to help him.

Except Tim.

Tim rushed over, kicked Phelps's legs out from under him, sending him to the ground. Then he straddled the burning man's chest, keeping him down while he rocked him on the ground, smothering the flames.

Fallows watched with his pale, colorless eyes. "We'll take a five-minute break here. If anybody wants to tend to Phelps, fine. If not, fine. Hey, Phelps."

There was a choked gasp from Phelps. "Yes."

"Be ready to march in five minutes or we leave you behind."

Phelps struggled to pull himself to a sitting position. Fallows never left anybody behind who was still alive.

"Follow me, Tim." Fallows marched off into the woods without looking back. Tim followed. They kept walking until they reached a small clearing. Fallows unpacked his binoculars and began scanning the sky. "Nothing yet."

Tim stood there without speaking. He'd decided that Fallows only used conversation to confuse him, to trick him somehow. With Fallows it was best to say nothing. Just wait for a chance to grab one 9mm bullet. Just one. Then he'd have plenty to say.

Fallows's head was tilted back, swiveling from side to side, adjusting the binoculars. "That damn Long Beach Halo. It's something all right. Almost pretty if you didn't know what was in it. What it could do to you. Right, Tim?"

"Yes." That was as much as he'd give the bastard. But it was true. The orange and yellow was pretty. But they'd seen a few people who'd tried to sail through it to the other side, despite the flyers that had warned everybody not to try or they'd be shot. The outside world was frightened of contamination. Tim didn't blame them. The ones he'd seen who'd been exposed to the Halo had gnarled, melted skin all over their bodies, their eyes half hanging out of the sockets. Those were the lucky survivors. Most died right away.

Tim looked around him, studying every bush and tree, looking for his father hiding out there somewhere. It was something he always did, searching. But lately, he'd been doing it a little less. Where was he after all this time?

"You did well back there, Tim," Fallows said, stuffing the binoculars back in their case. "With Phelps. Saving his life. Fast thinking."

Tim shrugged. "I didn't think. I just did it, that's all."

"That's a good sign. Quick reactions. You think that will make those men like you a little more? Treat you better?"

"I haven't thought about that." But he had. He'd hoped they would see how he'd helped one of them. Maybe he could turn that to his advantage sometime. Get one to help him escape, or at least make them watch him less closely. Make it easier for him to get that single 9mm bullet he wanted. "Like I said, I just did it."

"Sure. A humanitarian, like your dad. Come here. I want you to see something." Fallows plucked the binoculars from their case again and handed them to Tim. He put his hand on the boy's shoulder and pointed back toward the camp. "There. Take a look."

Tim pressed the cold glass against his eyes and lifted the binoculars in the direction of Fallows's finger. He saw Phelps still sitting on the ground, trying to pull himself to his feet by clawing up the side of a tree.

"What do you see?" Fallows asked. His tone suggested he already knew, even though Tim was sure he hadn't looked before. He'd kept his eyes on the sky. "Well?"

"Everybody's taking a break like you told them to. Smoking cigarettes or chewing tobacco. A couple of 'em are playing cards, blackjack I think."

"What about Phelps?"

"He's getting up. Looks OK."

"Anybody helping him?"

Tim hesitated. At first he'd thought they were just letting him climb to his own feet, like his father had made him do when he'd been thrown from his dirt bike. But Tim remembered the anxious look in his father's eyes, too. He'd wanted to rush over and hold his son, Tim could see that. But he wouldn't. Not until Tim got up and climbed back on that dirt bike. But these men were ignoring Phelps as if he were somehow unclean.

"I asked if anybody was helping Phelps. Giving him a hand, offering to tend to his wounds."

"No."

"Good. They've learned well."

Tim knew Fallows was waiting for a reaction. He didn't give him one. He just handed the binoculars back and waited.

Fallows smiled. "Yeah, you're Eric's kid all right. Same stubborn independence. There's a story I told your dad back in 'Nam when he was under my command. We'd just stormed a VC camp and I'd ordered my men not to take any prisoners. Well, one dumb ox from Baltimore hauls out this woman, couldn't have been more than seventeen. He asks me what he should do with her. I said, Shoot her in the head. He balked, his mouth hanging open like I'd ordered him to rape his mother. So I look around at the rest of my men and see that many are just as shocked as this Baltimore jerk. Fine, I thought. Let 'em learn a little lesson. OK, I told him, you can guard her. That night she gets hold of a knife and slices the Baltimore kid's throat. I see her sneaking out of camp and blow her head off with my .45. You see, I tell them, that's why we don't take prisoners. That night your daddy brings me the knife she'd used to shave the kid. He looks at me with those flat, ball-bearing eyes of his and says, handing me the knife, 'You lost something.' Yeah, your daddy knew right away it was me who slipped that bitch the knife." Fallows laughed. "Your dad was sharp, damn it. I'll give him that. So I told him to sit down, I've got a story to tell him. He says he'll stand. Stubborn bastard, like you. When I was a kid, I tell him, my friends and I used to hunt lizards. One day I caught about seven of them. I put them all in a cardboard box. That night I thought I'd feed them, so I caught this giant black bug, I didn't know what kind it was, and dumped it in the box with the seven lizards. Not much to eat, but I figured it would hold them until morning. When I came out the next morning I looked in the box and saw the black bug sitting on the back of one of the lizards. He'd eaten right through its back. He tried to crawl away, but the bug kept eating the red, gooey insides. The other six lizards were lying in the corners of the box with their backs turned." Fallows fixed his pale eyes on Tim. "What was I to learn from that sight?"

"That if all the lizards had banded together, they could have killed the bug."

"That's what your dad said. And if you look at it from the lizard's point of view you're right. But if you look at it from the bug's point of view, you see that the lesson is to keep everyone divided, break down their loyalties, and you can survive in a box full of lizards."

Tim stared at Fallows. "What did my father say to that?"

"Nothing. He got up and walked away." There was a look in Fallows's eyes, Tim thought, almost of great loss. Some color came back to them as he stared off. "I tried to teach Eric everything I knew. Make him into a friend. I don't know why I chose him. Something about him, something different. There are ways to make money during a war, lots of ways. I offered them to your father. He refused. No moral speeches about right and wrong. Just refusal. Somehow that was even worse. But later, when he testified against me at my court-martial, that was too much. Naturally I had to kill him. The lesson of the lizard, I'm afraid."

"But your men. Phelps."

"They won't help him. They won't help each other unless I order it. Each individual is a disposable unit, like a tissue. The only thing keeping them together is me. And that only works because I know how to get them what they want. So you see, we all need each other, but we don't need anybody."

Tim didn't know what to say. Talking with Fallows was confusing, exhausting. He was safer when he just concentrated on killing the man.

Fallows patted Tim's head. "'Tut! I have done a thousand dreadful things/As willingly as one would kill a fly.' *Titus Andronicus*, Act IV, scene iv, line 82. Are you familiar with Shakespeare?"

"Some. Dad used to read him to us sometimes. For every movie we went to see we had to read one book."

"Admirable. Perhaps you'd like to read some of the books I have?"

Tim backed off a few steps. "Why are you being nice to me now?"

"For the same reason I do everything. It suits me. And it's time you stopped peering at every rock and tree thinking your dad will pop out to take you back. If by some chance he isn't dead, he will be soon enough. Besides, he has a new woman and they'll start a new family. One that won't include you. He probably can't even remember what you look like. I'm the only who'll take care of you, Tim. And I will teach you everything you need to know. More than he did. You're my son from now on. Get used to it."

Tim thought it over for a few minutes, watching Fallows's craggy face, the bristly white hair like a field of snow-covered shrubs. When Tim spoke, his voice was cold and passionless. "I will kill you someday."

Fallows smiled. "Good. At least you have a goal. Not like a lot of kids these days."

He lead Tim back toward the camp, confident that within weeks the kid would be his. His alone.

"Colonel!" one of his men yelled from the camp. "Up there! Look!"

Fallows shaded his eyes with one hand and looked up into the sky. When he saw it, he just nodded. "Jesus Christ."

10.

Tracy hobbled toward the house, her makeshift crutches spearing yellow flyers as she walked. She stopped ten feet from the open doorway and shook one of the flyers loose from her right crutch. The big red letters exclaiming EVACU-ATE caught her eye and she felt her skin ice over. What if Eric was wrong? What if they really were going to drop those chemicals here today? But as she neared the house, the bitter, rotting smell smothered all other thoughts.

Except one. Why had Eric's bow been fired?

"Hey, Eric."

The answer came from somewhere inside the house. "Yeah?"

"How about I wait out here? Leg's a little weak. Not to mention the stomach." If he hesitated, or told her to come in anyway, she'd know he was in trouble. What would she do then? "OK with you?"

"Sure," he said. Tracy sighed with relief. "It's pretty gruesome in here anyway."

"I'll be right in."

Tracy negotiated the three steps in a hurry, knocking aside the front door with a crutch. Inside, the smell was even worse. She brought her hand with the gun up to cup over her nose. The scent of gun oil helped kill the harsher odor a little. Not enough.

The living room was as modest as the outside of the house. Home-made curtains, an old but well-tended sofa with doilies on each arm. A large studio photograph of a middle-aged couple and their teen-aged sons with their mother's pronounced overbite hung over the brick fireplace. Next to the fireplace was a pile of boards with nails still poking through the splintered wood where it had been torn apart. A thin layer of dust and ashes covered everything.

"Where are you?" Tracy asked.

"Bedroom. Just follow the flies."

"Flies? I thought they were crows." She waved a fat black one out of her face and leaned one crutch up against the wall. Resting her weight on the left crutch, she raised her .357 and limped forward to find Eric.

The flies were everywhere now, buzzing throughout the house like a crowd of gossiping crones. They flicked from room to room in hungry swarms with no fear of Tracy. She brushed them out of her face and off her hair as she followed Eric's voice down the narrow hallway into the far bedroom. By the time she reached it, she was gagging on the horrid smell. She tugged her shirt up over her nose.

"God almighty, Eric."

Eric nodded solemnly. "Yeah, I know."

His red kerchief was tied around his face like a bandit. The number of flies was staggering, huge, black clouds drifting around the room, humming like a chain saw, raining down plump, black flies onto the bed. And the man lying on it. At least she thought it was a man.

Next to the bed in a puddle of fresh blood with a crossbow bolt sticking out its chest, sprawled a gray German shepherd, his teeth bared and flecked with chunks of flesh. Clamped in his stiff, dead mouth was half a human foot, torn loose from the corpse on the bed. Eric planted his foot on the chest of the dog and yanked his arrow free, wiping the blood on the bedspread.

"This is probably the dog that made those tracks," Eric said. "He'd just started his meal when I came in. His name's Ralph."

"The man?"

"No, the dog." He bent over the dog and showed her the collar. MY NAME'S RALPH. CALL (213) 456-9080. "That's a Malibu prefix. He's come a long way."

Tracy hated knowing the dog's name. "Did you have to kill him?"

Eric gave her a look. "He didn't even bother dropping that foot when he came at me. It's going

106

to be hard to keep these animals happy with Gainesburgers anymore."

Tracy turned back to the corpse on the bed. Missing half a foot was the least of his losses. The right side of the face had been chewed off. She could still see the teeth marks where the flesh had been ripped off. He was also missing a leg and both arms, though their removal seemed neater, like the bodies back in Santa Carlotta. Flies dove at the open wound of his face, feasted, then flew away to be replaced by other flies. Tracy waved them all away with a pillow from the floor. But when she looked back at the face she saw the wound was moving. She looked closer. Clumps of tiny, white maggots squirmed inside the man's face. A couple crawled across what was left of his eyeballs.

Eric put an arm around her shoulder. "Looks like our friends from Santa Carlotta were here. Managed to take a leg and two arms."

"Christ, you make it sound like they were out shopping. Wings and thighs, extra crispy."

"Well, they were. I think they scavenge the bodies, eating what they can and carrying some back to the others."

She fought the tightening at her throat, the heaving in her stomach. "You mean, they killed him and then butchered him?"

"They didn't kill him. He was already dead."

Tracy looked at the body again. Of course. She'd sat through enough trials back when she sketched them for a living to notice there was almost no blood on the bed. Therefore the wounds had occurred after death.

"Then what happened?"

Eric shrugged. "I'm only guessing. But look at the hair. He's practically bald."

"So? A lot of men are."

"Yeah, but his is wispy here and there. Notice that photograph over the fireplace? This is the father. He's got all his hair there and the picture's dated two years ago."

"Maybe he had cancer."

"Maybe. But there are three graves out back that suggest his family died of something else. Problem is, the graves have been dug up. They're empty. Come on." He lead her back down the hallway to the living room. He squatted next to the fireplace, examining the half-burned boards among the ashes. Brushing his hands on the thighs of his jeans, Eric stood up and shook his head. "Arsenic poisoning."

"Pardon me, Inspector Ravensmith of Scotland Yard. Are you saying someone poisoned him or he poisoned his family and then himself?"

"Neither. It's the wood." He grabbed a board from the pile next to the fireplace and showed it to Tracy. "They probably scavenged this wood from some other home somewhere, maybe one that was destroyed in the quake. Been burning it for months now, using it for warmth and light and cooking."

"So?"

"So most lumber for outdoor use is treated with a preservative, chromate copper arsenate. When

108

you burn it, you get fumes, smoke, and ashes loaded with arsenic, plus chromium and copper. That combination will eventually kill you. But not before you lose your hair, get muscle cramps, diarrhea, headaches, earaches, and bronchitis."

Tracy tossed the wood back onto the pile of lumber. "Let's get out of here, OK?"

"He's got a hand pump rigged up to his own well. Plenty of fresh water."

"OK. We fill up the canteens first."

He raised one eyebrow. "I was thinking more along the lines of a bath."

"A bath? Jesus, Eric. Here?"

"Sure here. Maybe you haven't noticed, but your twenty-four-hour deodorant quit working about three months ago. My clothes are soaked through from that cesspool I was swimming in the other night and yours are three pounds heavier from the dirt and sweat. I say we make a campfire outside, heat some water, wash our clothes, and take our first hot bath in months. How's that sound?"

Tracy was surprised. At first, she thought she'd be revolted by the idea. Bathing while the owner's mutilated corpse rotted in a heavy coat of flies and maggots. It seemed horrible. But then again, the idea of hot water, of feeling scrubbed, of clean clothing was intoxicating. She was as excited as she might have been before the quake if she'd just won a million dollar lottery. Priorities change, she reminded herself.

"OK," she said. "Let's get naked."

Outside in the back yard, Eric stood bare-chested next to the tub and poured a bucket of steaming water around Tracy's naked body. The steam swirled into her face.

"Too hot?" he asked.

"No such thing. More, slave, or you shall feel my wrath."

"Without delay, Your Royal Boniness." Eric used one of Tracy's crutches to snag the handle of the second pail and lifted it off the fire. He tested the water with his finger before pouring it over her back.

"Oh God, yes." She leaned her head back to let the last half of the water stream over her short red hair. "I'm starting to think hot water will replace sex."

Eric laughed. "Just remember, nobody heats water the way I do, baby."

Tracy leaned back against the metal tub, closed her eyes, and sighed.

Eric peeled his pants off and dunked them into the clothes tub with Tracy's clothing. The hot water was already brown with dirt.

"No starch in mine," she said.

Eric climbed into the big, metal tub with Tracy, careful not to disturb her bandaged leg which was elevated into a sling he'd rigged over the tub. His body throbbed with gratitude as it felt the hot water wash over it. He dangled his hand over the side, felt the reassurance of his crossbow leaning there. Saw Tracy's .357 resting in the sling with her leg. Now he could relax.

Tracy lifted her good leg up and prodded his chest with her toes. "Look at all those scars. As if someone played tick-tack-toe on your chest."

He leaned forward, placed a finger on her left breast. "What about this?" His finger traced the three-inch scar that arched over her nipple, the result of an unknown sniper in Pasadena.

"Oh yeah? What about this? Looks like the fossil of some snake." She wound her fingertip along the eight-inch scar that twisted across his chest. A fall from a sheer cliff he'd been climbing had left him with two broken ribs and this scar.

He caught her fingers in his fist. "We can waste a lot of time counting scars. Visible and otherwise."

"Yeah." She pulled his hand to her lips and kissed his knuckles. Her foot skiied along his body until the arch was snug against his crotch. "Need soaping, mister?"

"We don't have any soap."

"Don't we?" She held up her empty hand, cupped around an imaginary bar of soap. "My favorite brand."

He nodded at her leg. "You'll hurt yourself."

"Only if I'm lucky."

Their hands explored each other lazily, kneading and massaging hard muscles at first. Tracy loved to have him squeezing her muscles, knowing they were firm and sinewy. Her body had chanced so much since the quakes. It had been curvy and thin before, but now it felt different to her. Powerful and practical. Completely within her control. Even the broken leg didn't bother her all that much. Once she would have yelped and whined about it, now she treated it as an adversary, easily conquered.

Eric's body had changed too. He'd been hard and muscular before, but now he was quicker, stronger. His reactions were instantaneous. She could especially feel the difference when they made love. His self-control was absolute. Delightful, rapturous. Sometimes even a little scary.

She let her hand slide along his hard thigh until she had hold of his solid penis. She squeezed slightly, felt the warm blood inside him pulse.

Eric's hand swooped between her legs, raking through her pubic hairs, then dipping into the exposed folds. He rubbed here, tapped there, toyed with her until she was wiggling along the bottom of the tub, thrusting herself onto his hand.

They looked into each other's eyes as they continued. They hardly ever closed their eyes anymore during sex. Instead they studied each other. It was as if they were checking to make sure the person was the same, that the world hadn't changed them too much. Tracy thought of it in terms of the old *Invasion of the Body Snatchers*, when Kevin McCarthy comes back and kisses Dana Wynter, only to find she'd been taken over while he'd been gone.

"This is going to be difficult," Eric said, sliding closer to her. Water slapped the edges of the tub.

"Necessity is the mother of invention. Start inventing."

Eric reached under her buttocks and lifted her up, sliding his hips directly under her. Slowly he lowered her onto his penis. With one hand, Tracy guided him into her.

Their movements were slow at first, a tender grinding against each other. Tracy's broken leg hurt a little, then the pain was replaced by a tingling of nerves. Sweat from the hot water and activity slicked her face, dripped into her eyes. Her mouth was partially open as she bit her lower lip.

Eric watched her green eyes, the lids heavy yet open. She didn't say anything, didn't try to act sexy. She didn't have to. It was all there in every swivel of her hips, the impish grin, the demanding eyes. He picked up the pace, his hands clamped on her hips as he lifted her slightly and brought her back down again. And again. And again.

He inhaled a lungful of steam mixed with Tracy's own musky scent. Not the scent of a city woman who shopped at Macy's or Bloomingdale's and finished each work day at some Happy Hour. It was the tangy scent of pure energy and desire. When he brought his hips up against hers again he felt his penis reaching even deeper inside. The muscles of her vagina tugged at him, pulled him into her. The pace increased.

Her long nipples rubbed against his chest as they bounced in the water, scars brushing scars. Then the heat began bubbling from somewhere inside him.

"Better come now before you bust my other leg," she said, her eyes fluttering, her face taut

113

with pleasure.

Eric drove into her. She gasped, squeeled, gripped his hair in her fist. He drove into her again. Her eyes closed, her teeth clenched. "Now, damn it," she pleaded. *"Now!"*

He bucked up while forcing her hips downward. His penis spurted like a lawn sprinkler. They hugged each other close, claws buried in flesh, while they rode out Eric's continued spasms.

They separated, Eric arranging Tracy so that her leg was comfortable. They both leaned back against opposite ends of the tub. Tracy's eyes were closed. She wiped sweat from her face and smiled. Eric stared up into the orange sky.

"Holy Christ!" he said.

Tracy grinned. "Thanks."

"Not you. That. Up there!"

They both stared up at the sky, their mouths slightly open.

11.

Everyone was strapped tightly into their form-fitted seats listening to Bill Weaver's nasal countdown through their helmets.

"Ten, nine, eight . . ."

Paige Lyons glanced over her shoulder at Dr. Bart Piedmont, who winked at her through his face plate and mouthed the word asshole at Weaver's whine. She laughed and turned back to check the five flight-control computers one more time.

". . . Six, five, four . . ."

At T minus five seconds, Paige felt the three main engines start up with a bang. Her insides swirled as if they were being pureed by some internal blender. The hell with what anybody said: This was always exciting. It was her third flight and she was wet between her legs now just as she had been the first two times. She'd been too embarrassed to tell anyone the first time it happened, even the flight physicians who wanted to know every damn thing. But later at a luncheon for a bunch of the old-time astronauts, she'd sneaked off to a bar with a few Mercury and Gemini astronauts where two of them confessed to having climaxed during takeoff. One said he thought he'd climaxed, but it turned out he'd just pissed his pants.

". . . Two, one, lift-off."

"Why don't they say 'blast-off?'" Piedmont complained. "It sounds more dramatic. Blast-off!"

The *Columbia* shook as the two solid-rocket boosters strapped to the big, white external tank exploded to life, lifting the craft on five columns of fire. Paige looked out the side window, watching the shuttle slide up the side of the tower like an express elevator. She hardly noticed the 160 decibels of racket outside.

"Hey," Piedmont said, "who farted?"

"We have *lift-off*!" Weaver yipped through the speakers.

"Blast-off!" Piedmont corrected him.

The *Columbia*'s tail was pointed south, so immediately after clearing the tower, it did its pre-programmed pitch and yaw maneuver to position itself east-northeast toward Gibraltar.

Jesus, Paige thought. Jesus, Joseph and Mary this feels so *good*!

"What's our altitude, Steve?" Paige asked.

"Just passed 170 thousand feet."

"Jettison solids."

"Right."

Paige pictured what was going on down on the Florida launch pad right now. The force of the blast-off would knock down several hundred feet of wire fence strung to keep the spectators back. Any grass within a mile of the launch pad would be seared. Buildings within a three-mile radius would be rocked. The thousands of people who'd gathered for this seven a.m. flight would have their heads all bent back staring up into the early morning sun as they watched the spaceship disappear behind a six-hundred-foot tail of flame.

Within two minutes and eleven seconds after lift-off they were twenty-nine nautical miles high. A bright, yellow-orange flame brushed across their windows. Six-tenths of a second later it was gone, along with the solid rockets. Eight booster separator motors had flared up and fired the solids off into the Atlantic.

Dr. Bart Piedmont was singing. "The joint is jumpin', it's really jumpin'."

"Give us a break, huh, Bart?" Steve said, annoyed.

Paige looked over her shoulder at Bart Piedmont, who was sticking his tongue out at Steve's back, panting and holding his hands up like the paws of a dog. Paige laughed again and Steve whirled angrily to look at Bart. By now Bart had on his serious scientist expression, as he intoned, "Two minutes to MECO."

"Check," Paige said. She glanced at the other

two passengers, Daryl Budd and Phil La Porte. They remained silently strapped in their seats. They weren't really astronauts, merely Special Forces soldiers specially trained for this mission. Both were twenty-seven years old, with lean, hard bodies. During their special space training sessions they'd maintained serious expressions despite the usual tension-easing kidding among the astronauts. But she had to admit, they'd learned fast and never once complained. Right now they were gripping their seats with clenched fingers, grinding their teeth as if they feared the entire craft would explode at any moment.

"This is Mission Control in Houston. Press to MECO."

Paige relaxed as the MECO, main engine cut off, kicked into place. If they'd gotten that far, there was no turning back now. *Columbia* leveled off the trajectory and Paige could see the earth through the window. This was her third time with such a view and it never was anything less than startling. The curvature of the earth against the black velvet of space. The various shades of ocean water. The blue shimmer at the top of the atmosphere.

"Jesus," Bart Piedmont gasped. "I didn't know."

Like the two soldiers from Special Forces, it was his first flight.

Paige didn't have any more time for sightseeing. In less than four minutes they'd have to jettison the external tanks. Pieces of white insulation from the tank were drifting by the windows like chips of ice. Routine.

The ship was flying upside-down underneath the tank to make getting away from it easier. The main engines cut off and the computers activated a sixteen-second separation sequence. The umbilical propellant lines were yanked out of the tank and back into the orbiter. Explosives blew the bolts fastening them to the tank.

The *Columbia* was flying free.

Soon the tank would begin its downward trajectory. Whatever pieces survived the atmospheric heat would plunge into the Indian Ocean.

"Are we free?" Paige asked, but she could see the three red lights wink out as well as Steve.

He pointed to them anyway. "Guess so."

There was no feeling of motion, no sense of the explosions firing. Paige took the stick and began manually flying off to the side to make sure they didn't run into the tank as it fell. The orbiter had forty-four reaction control engines, thrusters that allowed her to maneuver the direction and attitude of the craft while in space. She veered to the side and the computer fired off one thruster on the nose and one aft. The spacecraft shook violently as if hit by a meteor. Thirty-foot spears of fire leaped from the thrusters.

Paige grabbed the rotational hand controller and pulled up the *Columbia*'s nose. She jabbed a button and the two large OMS (orbital maneuvering system) engines, sitting above the main engines at the rear, fired. The ship was urged smoothly into orbit. About twenty minutes later

119

the OMS engines were fired again to keep the orbit circular.

Now they were sailing 130 miles above the earth.

Paige unbuckled her belt first. Fortunately she'd taken a motion-sickness pill before takeoff, just as the others had. Some of the earlier astronauts had found themselves too spacesick in zero gravity to do any work for a couple of days. She didn't have that kind of time.

She floated to the aft deck to open the doors that cover the payload bay. The doors had to remain open during most of the time in orbit so their built-in reflectors could radiate into space all the heat that built up from the massive electronic equipment aboard.

Steve and Bart were busily entering data into the computers. Bart was moving very carefully, trying to get used to the weightlessness. He looked like someone walking barefoot on a bed of nails.

"How'd the tiles do?" Steve asked.

Paige peered at the dark patches on the pod housing the OMS engine. "Missing a few. Nothing serious."

"RTV?"

The RTV was the red compound used to bond the heat-shielding tiles to the craft. The compound itself could insulate against heat up to nine hundred degrees. "Fine. We're just fine."

Paige looked at the two soldiers, still strapped tightly into their seats. They neither spoke nor looked around. Sweat had puckered their faces like acne. She felt a little sorry for them.

"How you boys doing?" Paige asked them.

"Fine, ma'am," Daryl Budd replied, his voice a little squeaky, his eyes wide while watching Paige float in front of him.

"Just fine, ma'am," Phil La Porte managed to choke out.

"Well, fine then, I guess." Paige floated back to her chair.

Bart Piedmont drifted past, starting to enjoy the sensation. "Hey, guys, how they hanging. Whoops. I suppose in zero gravity they aren't hanging at all, huh?" He laughed to himself as he checked one of the computers.

Steve looked disgusted. "You know, Piedmont, even if this mission isn't going out on TV, everything you say is still broadcast back to Houston Control."

"How they hangin', Houston?"

Muffled laughter filtered through the speaker from Houston. "Got a little static here, guys. Better check out your end."

"Will do, Houston," Paige said, grinning. Christ, Steve was even stuffier than before. Meat and potatoes, high school football letter, degree in engineering from the navy. All he wanted from her is to be his little cheerleader, forever young in her miniskirt. Thing was, sometimes that seemed almost appealing. Almost.

She felt the slight stinging in the crease of her index finger where she'd burned herself a couple of nights ago. She'd decided to bake a cake. It was a ritual she performed every few months, an attempt to do something culturally feminine. It was her way of thumbing her nose at those, even within her own family, who said, "Sure you can orbit the earth, but why can't you keep a man?" By choice, was her answer. But sometimes she felt that guilt, that doubt, that longing to fulfill the role expected of her. Last March after her thirty-third birthday, she'd felt it even more. If she was ever going to have a child, she'd have to decide soon, while it was still safe. It made her feel a little like a time bomb.

In the meantime, she proved herself by cooking a fancy Chinese dish, making an apron, taking ballroom dancing. This time it was baking a cake. She'd never done it before, but how hard could it be? She'd opened the cookbook. German chocolate seemed easy enough. Maybe too easy. She'd make it with coconut-pecan frosting. She methodically lined up all the ingredients she would need: flour, sweet cooking chocolate, buttermilk, pecans, coconut, etc. Everything in a neat row. Not only would she bake the fucking cake, she wouldn't even make a mess doing it.

Three hours later it was done. Perfect. Just like the lemon chicken, the apron, her dancing. And the kitchen was neater than when she'd started. Except for the tiny blister on her finger where she'd touched the hot pan while stirring the frosting. It seemed every time she took on one of these projects she injured herself in some small way. Not enough to be bothersome, but kind of like a reminder. She shook it out of her head.

Maybe it was this mission that brought out those questions. Thinking about her father. Not that he'd been anything but encouraging to her. Still, with her mother dead for the past eight years, her father was all she had left of a family. Maybe that's what kept her thinking about starting her own family. It didn't matter. Right now, only the mission mattered.

"California here we come," Bart was singing. Only this time, he wasn't smiling.

"We're going down," Paige said.

Capt. Steve Connors and Dr. Bart Piedmont scrambled back to their seats. The two soldiers, Daryl Budd and Phil La Porte, had never left their seats, hadn't even unbuckled their belts.

"You guys don't know what you're missing," Bart said as he swam through the air toward his seat. He pursed his lips and puffed in and out like a fish.

So far everything had gone perfectly. NASA needed film to supply to the news programs to convince them of the routine aspect of the flight, so for half an hour they'd all looked busy and professional for the onboard cameras. Even Bart had kept his joking clean. Budd and La Porte had been kept in the background as much as possible, and would probably be edited out later anyway.

"What's that?" Bart said, pointing out the payload bay. They were flying upside-down, as usual, which made the payload bay the best view.

Thick ribbons of red and brown and white swirled on the earth below. "Dasht-e Kavir," Paige said. "Salt desert in Iran."

"It's magnificent."

Paige nodded. "My favorite too. Except for the Amazon when there are thunderstorms."

"I prefer the Bahamas," Steve said. "Greener than a jealous woman's eyes." He chuckled at his own wit.

"But not greener than our two friends here," Bart said.

The speakers crackled. "You guys ready to de-orbit?"

"Ready, Houston," Paige answered.

"Pressure suits secure?"

"Check."

"Biomedical sensors strapped on?"

"Check."

"Payload doors closed?"

Paige flipped the switch. "Check."

"Computers programmed for re-entry?"

"Check."

There was a pause. "Got your maps to the stars' homes?"

Paige laughed. "And tickets to the *Tonight Show*."

"Then you're ready. Good luck, *Columbia*."

"Thank you, Houston."

Paige began the process of bringing the craft down from its speed of almost twenty-five times the speed of sound. She fired the OMS engines to slow them down to less than three hundred feet per second and push them into an elliptical orbit the low point of which would be closer to the earth's surface. When the OMS burn was over, she pitched the ship over so it was in a forty-degree nose-up angle that would let the insulated underbelly deal with the atmosphere's heat.

They hit the atmosphere at Mach 24.5 after passing Guam. Immediately they lost radio contact with Houston since there were no tracking stations in that part of the Pacific. Also, the heat of re-entry would stifle any radio broadcasts for the next sixteen minutes.

Paige saw the blips of orange out of the corners of her eyes as the reaction-control jets fired. Five minutes after losing contact with Houston, they noticed the pinkish red glow as the thirty-one thousand chalklike square tiles made from pure Minnesota sand began to absorb the heat.

"Get those visors down," Paige commanded.

Everyone did.

The visors sealed the pressure suits so that they would automatically inflate if re-entry heat burned through the cabin and released the air.

"It doesn't feel hot in here," Bart said, amazement mixed with relief.

"It's not supposed to," Steve said.

"Here comes the tricky part," Paige announced.

They could see the dense huddle of gray clouds almost a thousand miles long just off the western coast of the United States. North America looked funny, not at all like the shape they all had etched in their memories. With California gone all the way from San Francisco to the Mexican Baja, North America now looked like a one-armed man. The clouds shrouding the island of California looked like an empty sleeve floating out to sea. They could even make out the tiny dots that were navy patrol boats preventing anyone from entering or exiting that fog.

"Christ," Steve Connors said. "You're the scientist, Bart. You sure we're going to be safe going through that thing? You've seen what it's done to the few who've gone through."

"Don't worry. We've got a special decontamination chamber onboard that should do the trick. Besides, the heat from re-entry should kill anything it touches."

"We've already gone over this, Steve," Paige said.

"Yeah, but that was sitting on our asses in Florida. I'm talking about a couple minutes from actually entering that crap. What happens when we take off again? We won't have that re-entry heat to protect us then?"

Bart sighed. "No, but we'll still have the decon chamber. The heat's just an extra bonus. So don't worry, you're perfectly safe." He paused. "Unless you've had sex within the last week."

"What?" Daryl Budd hollered.

"They didn't say nothing about that," Phil La Porte said.

"Sure they did, fellas. Told all us guys. Have sex and pass through the Halo, your dong drops off within the hour. Right, Dr. Lyons?"

Paige kept a straight face. "Absolutely, Dr. Piedmont."

"*Penis shrivelitis* is the technical term, I think," Bart continued.

"Knock it off, Bart," Steve said. "We've got work to do." He frowned at Paige. "Why do you encourage him?"

"I like him."

"Yeah, I bet you do."

Paige laughed. She'd forgotten Steve's ridiculous jealousy.

The computers had the shuttle doing rolls to slow it down as they slipped through the approach corridor. The thrusters were still firing. They did their last roll at Mach 2.6 and the thrusters stopped. They shifted to the all-aerodynamic mode.

Suddenly the windows were dark with the Long Beach Halo swarming around them. The orange-yellow of the Halo mixed with the orange-yellow of the re-entry heat. It was almost beautiful, like fireworks viewed through a thick fog. Then they were through it and could see the airfield where they were supposed to land.

Steve began calling out the air speeds so Paige didn't have to keep scanning the instrument panels as closely. "350 knots . . ."

Paige adjusted the pitch.

". . . 300 . . . 250 . . . 200 . . ."

The airstrip spread out before them like a rocky carpet. They'd been warned that it might not be in good shape. It wasn't. The quakes had buckled sections, cracked other sections.

"Doesn't look good," Steve said.

"There's enough good left to make it."

"You're the boss," he said sarcastically.

They touched down at 185 knots with only the slightest bump and rolled smoothly down the runway, rocking occasionally when they hit a crack.

"Great landing, Paige," Bart said.

Paige hit the radio switch. "Come in, Houston."

Static answered back.

"Well, now we know why we've never been able to establish radio contact with the survivors here."

Steve and Paige began flipping switches, shutting down systems.

Bart unbuckled himself and gestured to Budd and La Porte. "You two follow me. Once I'm decontaminated, you're next. Let's go."

When the systems were all secured, Steve and Paige unbolted the metal locker in the downstairs cabin. Steve pried open the lid and handed Paige a 9mm H&K P9S side arm. She strapped her holster on, slammed a full clip into the gun, and jammed the gun into the holster.

"Well," Steve said.

Paige shrugged. "Yeah, well."

The hunt was officially on.

12.

"So that's what they look like," Tracy said.

Eric nodded, drank from his canteen.

"It's different than I imagined. I don't know, bigger, I think. A lot bigger."

They laid belly-down in the rough weeds, their heads lifted just enough to peer at the parked *Columbia*. Not that there was anything suspicious to see. They'd only arrived an hour ago, but Eric calculated that the craft couldn't have touched down more than an hour before that. Still, there was no movement so far. No one had come out since they'd arrived.

Eric shaded his eyes with a folded yellow flyer. "Annie and I took the kids to Edwards Air Force Base to watch the *Columbia* land from its first flight. Runway twenty-three on Rogers Dry Lake."

"Must've been quite a show."

Eric smiled. "Yeah. The kids were kind of bored. Tim sulked because it meant missing a chess match and Jenny flirted with some boy whose parents had driven in all the way from Ohio. But Annie and I were acting like kids on our first date, staring up in the sky with our binoculars, nudging each other. Giggling. Funny, huh?"

Tracy felt that familiar surge of tenderness for him. And jealousy over Annie. Annie's dead, damn it, she wanted to scream. I'm not. And yet she didn't have the right. He treated her with love and respect. Still, there was something missing. That something he'd felt for Annie. "Yeah, funny."

Eric handed her the canteen. She took a swig.

"How much longer do we wait?"

He looked up at the sky. The Halo was darkening as night approached. "Should be dark enough soon. We can get closer then."

"Maybe they're already gone."

"I don't think so. They probably have to go through some medical process first to make sure the Halo didn't contaminate them."

Tracy handed the canteen back and sighed. "You think maybe they've got room for a couple more aboard that thing? Like when it takes off."

Eric looked at her, his smile gone, his eyes flat and cold. He didn't say anything, but she knew what he was thinking: He'd never leave without Tim.

"I didn't mean anything, Eric. Just daydreaming."

"I know, Trace. I know." He forced a smile for her.

They watched in silence for another forty minutes. The Long Beach Halo's bright orange-yellow haze faded into a dull gray night. A smear of faint light overhead marked the moon. But no stars. No universe outside this island.

"There," Tracy whispered excitedly, pointing.

A couple pairs of legs could be seen walking on the other side of the *Columbia*.

"Now what?" Tracy said.

Eric stood up with his crossbow. "Now we crash the party. Come on."

They started for the spacecraft.

Paige was the last through the decontamination chamber, a rather boring process made tolerable only by the fact that she'd brought along a copy of Miller's biography of Lyndon Johnson. It was the worst-kept secret among the astronauts that Paige had political ambitions once she left NASA. Some of the guys had taken to humming "Hail to the Chief" when she entered a room, but all in good fun. In the meantime, Paige immersed herself in political biographies, determined not to make the same mistakes others had made.

After everyone had been purified, changed and armed, Paige hefted her backpack onto her shoulders. She tightened the straps while Steve checked her belts and loops. Then he shrugged into his backpack and she checked his belts and loops.

"OK," Paige said, trying to keep the nervous excitement out of her voice, "this is it. Safari time."

Daryl Budd and Phil La Porte were already outside, securing the area. Each was armed with a laser-aimed HK 93.

Dr. Bart Piedmont leaned against his seat as he watched Steve and Paige check their side arms. Steve handed Paige a laser-aimed HK 93 and shouldered a Franchi SPAS 12 semiautomatic twelve-gauge shotgun.

"Nasty looking thing," Bart said, nodding at the SPAS.

"It'll do the job," Steve said.

"I've been thinking," Bart said, looking at Paige. "With the saturation of all those leaflets, I don't see where we'll have any trouble here. I think it would be a good idea if you took either Mutt or Jeff with you."

Paige shook her head. "You know the procedure, Bart."

"Yeah, but I also know that you have about forty-five hours left to find your father and/or his papers. Then I have to fly this bugger out of here. And I'm not nearly the pilot you are."

"That's for sure. Which is why I intend to be back with time to spare. I know where his cabin retreat is and all the best ways to get there. Hell, I spent a lot of summers up here with him. It's going to be a simple in-and-out operation. Trust me."

132

Bart smiled weakly. "Making campaign promises already, huh?"

"Practicing. Let's see how well I keep it. Meantime, you and the Hardy Boys down there are to keep this baby secure. Anyone comes near, don't ask them in for lunch. Kill them. Right?"

"Yeah, right."

"Besides, you'll have plenty to do while we're gone. NASA still expects you to collect data from the Halo and check out the environment. See if this place is even worth salvaging anymore."

Bart threw up his hands. "OK, OK. You two are on your own. Find Papa and get your ragged asses back. Seems quiet enough out there."

Paige and Steve started down the ladder to the ground.

Gunshots blasted through the night.

"Got him!" Daryl Budd hollered. "Fuckin' got him."

Eric had held his hands away from his body as he'd approached the *Columbia*, but his finger had still been hooked around the trigger of his crossbow. In less than a second he could snap the bow into place and fire the bolt. That was some small comfort.

The two men dressed in army fatigues and carrying HK 93s didn't see him immediately, so Eric called out to them. "Hey, fellas. I'm Sergeant Ben Turner, Air Force recruiter out of San Jose. Sure am glad to see you boys. It's been a hell of a—"

Eric watched them swivel toward him, their HK 93s at their shoulders, a tiny red light beaming into the night toward him. He looked down, saw the red dot slide across the grass in front of him, run up his pants leg, and rest right in the middle of his chest.

"Shit!" he barked and dove for the ground as a metallic chatter sounded. Bullets whizzed by, barely missing him. He glanced back and saw Tracy also flattened to the ground. "You OK?"

"Maybe they just don't like recruiters. You should've told 'em you were Ricardo Montalban and welcomed them to Fantasy Island."

"Hey!" Eric shouted at the men. "I don't know what your mission is, but you're about three or four hours from being attacked by a well-armed army of a dozen or so soldiers. You interested in details?"

There was a long silence, maybe five minutes.

"We're listening," replied a deep female voice.

Eric laughed harshly. "Gee, that's swell of you, but it doesn't quite work that way. We've got information. You want it, you buy it."

Another pause. "What do you want?" the woman asked.

"I don't know," Eric shouted back. "But we'll find something."

"Out of the question," Paige said. Her mouth was tight and her arms crossed, a pose that those who knew her realized meant she wouldn't budge.

Eric shrugged. "Suit yourself, Dr. Lyons.

I don't know what you are up to here in the Golden State, but I know when Colonel Fallows and his merry men come tramping through those woods, he's going to turn the *Columbia* into a swap meet of spare parts."

"We can handle him," Daryl Budd said, tugging his army hat lower over his eyes.

"Maybe," Eric said. "Maybe not. But I don't want to be in your place to find out." He stood up, gestured to Tracy to follow. She lifted her crutches.

"I'm not authorized to give you weapons, Mr. Ravensmith."

"Sure you are."

"What I mean is, we'll need them, especially if what you say about this Colonel Fallows is true."

"Oh, it's true. I know him." He touched the white scar along his jaw. "I know him very well. He wouldn't have been fooled by those government flyers' testing bullshit any more than I was."

"It's not bullshit, Ravensmith," Paige said. "We are here testing, trying to find a way to help all of you survivors. We just didn't want to be swamped by people trying to get us to take them back with us. You can understand that much, can't you?"

Eric shook his head. "Stick with the story if you want, it doesn't matter to me. Here's the deal though. I want one of those HK 93s and three banana clips. Then I might be able to help you with your problem."

Steve Connors stood up and shoved his SPAS shotgun against Eric's chest. "Fuck off, buster.

What you'll get is a hole in your chest as big as your mouth."

Eric knocked the barrel aside with his forearm, spun forward, and swung his elbow into Captain Connors's throat. The astronaut gagged, clutched his throat and dropped to his knees. By the time Budd and La Porte had lifted their guns, Eric had twisted the shotgun from Steve's hands and was pointing it at Paige.

"Yeah," Tracy said, climbing to her feet. "And if you've got any magazines, we'll take those too."

"It would be appreciated." Eric smiled.

Paige looked impatiently at her watch. "OK, OK. We don't have the time for this, so we'll level. We're on a mission to rescue somebody from here. We've got less than two days to find him and take off."

"Who is it?" Eric said.

Paige shook her head. "National security."

"Are you kidding me? Who are we going to tell?"

Bart Piedmont laughed. "He's got you there, Paige."

She shot Bart a stern look, then turned back to Eric. "OK. He's a scientist. Got something to do with armed satellites. That's all you need to know."

"What's his name?"

She hesitated, sighed. "Lyons. Dr. Ronald Lyons. Yes, we're related, he's my father. Happy?"

"For now," Eric said. "You have any idea where to look for him?"

"Some."

"But you're not going to tell me?"

Paige remained silent.

Eric walked around the *Columbia*'s large downstairs cabin, his fingers brushing control panels, furniture. It felt funny to be inside, touching everything that he and Annie had looked at through binoculars a few years ago. It made him miss her and he felt that bitter lump rising in his throat. That day as they'd watched she reminded him of what one astronaut had said once when asked what he thought about when orbiting the earth. And he'd said something like how he tried to ignore the fact that his capsule was built by the lowest bidder. Then she'd whispered something naughty in his ear and laughed and laughed. Eric swallowed the lump and smiled.

Steve Connors finally climbed to his feet, rubbing his sore throat, swallowing with great difficulty. He grit his teeth at Eric and said, "Gimme my damn gun, Ravensmith."

"First we reach our agreement."

"Like hell, asshole!"

"Shut up, Captain," Paige said. "What's your proposal, Ravensmith?"

"First, I take the HK 93, complete with laser-aiming device, of course."

"What else?"

"Well, this is the tricky part." He looked straight into Paige's stern eyes. "I want you to take a passenger back with you."

"No way!" Paige said. "Forget that. We'll do just fine without your help, mister. You and your lady can leave now."

"OK, but the moment we walk out of here, your mission is dead. And so are you. Haven't you ever heard of Colonel Dirk Fallows?"

"Wait a minute," Steve Connors said. "Fallows and Ravensmith. Sure, you guys were with that weird bunch, Night Shift. Did all the shit jobs, the clean-up jobs that even the Green Berets wouldn't do." He nodded his head with new respect. "Yeah, I heard of you over in 'Nam. He wiped out some civilian village and you ratted on him, got him thrown in military prison."

"You've got a good memory. Pilot?"

"Yeah. Mostly fighters, sometimes Caribou."

"What else did you hear?"

"That the whole Night Shift group were fugazi, every one of you a double veteran."

Eric laughed.

Dr. Bart Piedmont said, "You guys still speaking English? You flew a caribou, Steve? What's fugazi? A double veteran?"

Paige answered. "A Caribou is a small transport plane. Fugazi is military jive for fucked up. I don't know what a double veteran is."

Eric leveled his flat eyes on her. "It's a man who has sex with a woman and then kills her."

"Swell," she said.

"Now you know what you're up against. Fallows will wipe you out in ten minutes."

Paige looked at Steve, who remained uncharacteristically silent. Obviously he was impressed by this man, and that impressed Paige. Steve might be a pain in the ass, but he was a first-rate pilot and a good judge of everyone's character but his own. She'd have to be careful with the Ravensmith guy.

"OK, Ravensmith, what's your plan?"

"You and me and the pilot go out after your dad. That will leave, including Tracy, four people here to guard the craft."

"Wait a minute, Eric," Tracy protested.

"Now that's still not enough to defend this place, even with your weaponry. Not unless we even the odds by splitting Fallows's group."

"How do we do that?" Paige said.

"We'll deal with that detail later. Right now, we've got to get moving or it'll be too late."

Paige tilted her head and squinted at him. "Suppose we go along with this. You know damn well that this ship is computerized right down to the last pound of weight. Maybe, just maybe we can take a passenger like you ask, but there's no way we can take both of you. We couldn't take the weight." She paused. "So which one of you is going and which one of you is staying? You our passenger, Ravensmith?"

"Nope."

"Oh, so it's ladies first, huh? Your young friend then?"

"Neither of us." Eric walked over to Bart Piedmont. "Your passenger is male, about 120 pounds, almost five-foot-eight. Anything else you need to know?"

Bart Piedmont shrugged. "His name?"

"Tim Ravensmith."

"Where is he?" Paige asked.

"With Fallows. He was kidnapped. But he'll be

139

here at lift-off."

Paige shook her head. "We won't help you get him back."

Eric smiled. "I know."

"I just wanted you to know that up front. We've got to understand each other right now."

"Oh, I think we understand each other, Dr. Lyons. Don't we?"

Paige didn't answer. "OK, everyone outside except Ms. Ammes. You can stay there for the time being. Once we're gone, though, I want this area secured with everything we've got."

"Including the mines?" Phil La Porte asked.

"Especially the mines." She grabbed Bart Piedmont's arm. "Go on, get out of here. Dr. Piedmont and I are checking out the flight deck upstairs first."

Eric walked over to Tracy, kissed her gently on the lips. She grabbed his shirt in her fist and pulled him down, crushing her lips against his. Everyone watched, the two soldiers exchanging winks, Steve Connors sulking from the humiliating blow Eric had given him, Bart Piedmont grinning, and Paige Lyons frowning, trying to ignore the warmth spreading along her hips and thighs.

"Take care, Eric."

"Sure," he said and led the others down the stairs.

Paige nudged Bart up the ladder to the flight deck. When they were upstairs, she closed the hatch to make sure they couldn't be heard. "Well," she asked him, "what do you think?"

"I think that we're lucky that guy happened along. Otherwise we'd probably all be dead by the time you returned."

"If he's telling the truth."

"Come on, Paige. You know he is."

"Yeah, probably."

Bart sighed, a grim look clenching his features. "You know our fuel situation, Paige. The computers are programmed to take off with only four people aboard. You, Steve, me and your father. The plan all along has been to leave Budd and La Porte behind, even though they don't know it. There's no way we can take the kid."

"I know."

"So what are you going to do? He's not the kind of man who'll let you back out of a deal."

"I know, Bart. I don't know what I'll do." She shook her head. "Kill him, I guess."

13.

Fallows leaned against the pine tree and flipped the 9mm bullet into the air, caught it, flipped it up again. Tim squatted on the ground next to him, watching.

The rest of Fallows's men were making camp, following their routine silently, aware that Fallows was observing each one of them even when it looked like he wasn't. But even when the men were sure they were alone, they didn't complain. What for? Fallows might be the meanest bastard alive, but he was also the smartest. They lived better than any of the scum they'd come across in their travels. And there wasn't one thing that Fallows wanted that he hadn't managed to take. Who else on this damn island could make that claim?

"Catch," Fallows said, and flipped the bullet to Tim.

Tim caught it with one hand, opened his palm as if he wasn't sure he'd really caught it after all. But, yes, there it was. A 9mm bullet. A perfect match for his Walther. He didn't do anything with it, though. He watched Fallows, waiting for the trap.

"Smart kid." Fallows grinned, mussing Tim's hair.

Tim didn't budge. Fallows had taken to doing that a lot lately, mussing his hair or patting his back or hugging his shoulder. For the first time, these had become more frequent than the punches, bruises and burns. He didn't understand what Fallows was up to, but he knew it was something. Something creepy.

Tim examined the bullet sitting in the palm of his dirty hand like a jewel set in leather. He considered trying to load the bullet and shooting Fallows, but he knew he wasn't fast enough. He remembered Fallows's hard fingers wrapped around his own, forcing him to squeeze the trigger, forcing him to kill that man Dobbs. It had bothered him a lot at the time, not so much anymore.

"I want you to keep that bullet," Fallows was saying. "Keep it in your pocket. I don't ever want to see you loading that into your gun. You know I'll catch you if you try. Then I'll have to punish you. Right?"

"Right."

Fallows placed his foot against Tim's back.

"Huh? I didn't hear you."

"Right, sir."

Fallows kicked Tim's back, sending him sprawling forward into the dirt. A few men glanced over their shoulders at them, but no one said anything.

Fallows had his heavy combat boot on the back of Tim's neck, pinning the boy's head to the ground. "Say what, Tim?"

"Right, sir."

"Louder."

"Right, sir!"

"Louder." He leaned his weight on Tim's neck. Tim moaned. "Louder, son."

"Right, sir!"

Fallows leaned back against the pine tree, lifting his foot from Tim's neck. His voice was calm, pleasant. "That's better. Now put the bullet in your pocket."

Tim slowly dragged himself to his knees. Dirt was smeared on the side of his face, powdered on his lips. He opened his fist and the bullet was still there. He shoved it into his pocket.

"And keep it there. One day I'm going to tell you to load it into your gun. But that's not until I'm certain that you know who your real benefactor is. Understand?"

Tim nodded. With the bullet out of sight, he didn't think about it anymore. He didn't think about his father or Fallows or escaping or anything. It was funny, but he wasn't even mad at Fallows for kicking him or stepping on him or anything. He hardly ever felt mad anymore. Or happy. Or anything. Sometimes he'd think about his mother, but not as much anymore. Sometimes he even had trouble remembering what she looked like. Another funny thing, sometimes Fallows would have to go off and do something and he'd leave Tim with a guard. Weird thing is, once or twice lately when that happened, Tim kind of missed Fallows. Not because he liked him or anything, it was more like: At least he was familiar; Tim knew what to expect. And Fallows talked to him all the time. Crazy talk, Tim used to think, only now he didn't know anymore. Maybe not so crazy.

"Hey, Ryan," Fallows yelled. "Get your ass out to the south perimeter and relieve Jose. Son of a bitch is likely to stay there all day."

"Right, Colonel," Ryan half-saluted with his M-16 and jogged off into the woods. Fallows was right about the big Mexican. He wouldn't budge unless Fallows told him to. He was a couple inches past six feet, used to fight as a heavyweight in Vegas and Atlantic City. Pounded the shit out of a couple contenders for a few rounds, but could never go the distance. Had white man's legs, they'd said, no endurance. But he was loyal to Fallows. Too dumb to be anything else.

"Jose." No answer. "Hey, Martinez." Ryan saw the huge bulk sitting up in the tree, his camouflage hat pulled low over his face, his carbine cradled in his arms. He didn't stir. "Asshole," Ryan muttered. He picked up a stone from the ground and hurled it at Jose. The rock popped off the trunk a foot from the Mexican.

"When I tell Fallows you was sleeping, man, he's gonna stuff your burrito, partner."

No reply.

Ryan walked up to the tree, slung the M-16 over his shoulder, and hung on one of the low branches, letting his weight shake the tree.

The big man in the tree stirred. "Hey, man?"

Ryan dropped from the branch and looked up. "Hey, man, your ass. Time for you to get back to camp, *amigo*."

But Jose just waved a hand at him, jamming his hat even further down on his face. That wasn't like Jose. Camp meant food to Jose, and no one in his right mind stood between Jose and food.

Ryan started to unsling his M-16, felt a stinging at the back of his neck, looked down in time to watch something slick with blood burst through his throat, and yank his whole body forward a few inches where the arrow stuck into the trunk of the pine tree, pinning his neck to the tree. Ryan tried to talk, but that only forced the air through the hole in his neck. Pink bubbles foamed around the arrow shaft and his throat. With what little strength he had left, he tried to pull his neck free from the arrow. He couldn't. The life drained from his legs, arms, chest. Everything turned heavy, petrified. He passed out and the weight of his body pulled the arrow out of the tree as he fell. He died seven seconds later.

Steve Connors removed Jose's cap and climbed out of the tree. Paige appeared from behind a tree where she wiped the blade of her knife with a leaf. She left Jose's body behind the tree with the throat slit. Well, she'd been able to kill a man after all.

Eric approached from behind another tree, his crossbow loaded again. "That should get their attention."

"Then what, hotshot?" Steve said.

"Then they either split up, one group following us and the other continuing on to the shuttle. . . ."

"Or?" Paige asked.

"Or they all follow us. Either way, that gives the shuttle a chance to still be there when we get back."

"If they haven't caught us."

"At least we'll be able to move," Eric said. "And they don't know where we're going. That plane can't go anywhere. And neither can the people in it. Not for another forty hours."

Paige nodded. They'd been through this before. She didn't like it, but she had to admit it was the best plan they had. This Ravensmith knew what he was doing. Jesus, that's odd, her hands were beginning to shake. She felt funny, tingly, a little faint.

"You OK, Paige?" Steve asked, putting an arm around her.

She shook it off. "Fine, Captain Connors. Let's go." Thing was, though, her feet felt cold, numb.

"You ever kill before, Dr. Lyons?" Eric asked.

She didn't answer. There hadn't been a choice at the time. Ravensmith had gone ahead to scout while she and Steve had taken the south approach. They'd been creeping along quietly when they'd spotted the Mexican climbing down the tree. Steve had signaled for her to wait behind for him and she hadn't argued. The Mexican stretched his legs out, pissed on the side of the tree, and started to climb up again.

Steve sneaked up to the tree, clamping his knife in his teeth like some boyish pirate. Paige thought he looked silly, but realized they couldn't afford to have a gun go off and warn the rest of Fallows's men. Not just yet.

When the Mexican had one leg on the lowest branch, Steve sprung out at him, thrusting the knife straight at the Mexican's barrel chest. But Jose twisted away in time and the knife only managed to slice through his left arm. The carbine dropped from Jose's hand to the ground below.

Steve thrust again. Jose caught Steve's wrist and yanked it hard. The knife plopped next to the carbine. Jose jumped from the tree, his hand still crushing Steve's wrist. With his left fist, Jose punched Steve's jaw twice. Steve fell to the ground, stunned. Jose was angry, too angry to worry about the gun or knife on the ground. He just wanted to show this bastard what he used to do with his kind in the ring. He straddled Steve's chest and began pounding the smaller man with lefts and rights. His wounded arm didn't even hurt anymore. He didn't notice the woman until too late.

Not until she'd already grabbed a handful of his thick black hair, jerked his head back, and slid the knife across his neck. That didn't hurt either and he thought maybe she'd been too squeamish to actually cut him and he would teach her a lesson next, the whore. But then he found he couldn't get up and something was running down his neck like hot soup. She was pulling him off the other man and he was letting her. Fallows would be mad, he thought, dead before he even realized he was dying.

Eric had come back then and set up the scenario. She'd waited behind the tree while they'd finished off the other guy, amazed at how cool and composed she felt. Nonplused was a good word. But now. The shaking, the cold. Christ.

"Let's get moving," Eric said, a tenderness in his voice she hadn't expected. Steve was being soothing but not tender. He didn't know the difference. "You'll feel better if you keep active." Eric grinned at her. "Not that we have any choice. When one of them doesn't return to camp in the next few minutes, they'll come after him."

Paige nodded. "Then after us."

"Right." He hooked his hand under her arm to steady her.

"I've got her, Ravensmith," Steve Connors barked, grabbing Paige's other arm.

Paige shook them both free. "Nobody's 'got' me. Now let's get out of here."

They marched through the woods, through a clearing that arced up a hill. From the top of the hill they could see the rim of the forest where it bordered the fields. They'd also be able to see Fallows's men when they emerged.

"There they are," Paige said, counting the men

as they sifted through the trees into the clearing. Seventeen. More than she'd expected. They huddled in a circle around one tall man with white hair. Next to the man was a boy. Ravensmith's son, she realized. "What are they doing?"

"Deciding how many to send after me and how many after your shuttle."

"What do you think they'll do?"

"Depends," Eric said.

"On what?"

"On how badly Fallows wants me."

All seventeen men started through the clearing following the tracks Eric left for them.

"Well," Paige said, "I guess that answers that."

14.

Dr. Paige Lyons wrapped her arms around the skinny tree to keep from falling on her face. She bent over, expecting to vomit, but she was too tired even for that.

Next to her, Capt. Steve Connors hugged his stomach with one hand and pressed against his heart with the other, as if fearing it would burst through his chest. His mouth was open as he gasped for air.

"I thought astronauts were supposed to be in good shape," Eric said innocently.

"We . . . are," Steve said. "I've . . . run . . ." He started coughing.

"He's run . . . marathons," Paige said.

Steve nodded, held up two fingers. "Twice."

Paige pointed at herself. "Jog . . . every day."

"Gee," Eric said, "we've only run about eight miles. Hardly anything to a pair of sports like you."

Steve straightened up, his face glowing red. "Eight miles up and down goddamn hills. In the goddamn dark. Shit."

Paige slid to the ground, her back propped against the tree, her legs splayed straight out. "Well, you wanted them following us. Congratulations."

"Thanks." Eric tipped his canteen back and drank. "We're still a good forty minutes ahead of them. Pretty soon they'll stop for the rest of the night."

"Thank God," Paige said. "I'd sell my soul for a couple hours sleep."

"I said *they'd* stop for the rest of the night. Not us."

Steve Connors pointed an angry finger at Eric. "Listen, pal, we've been going along with you so far. But now you're starting to bug me. What's the point in all this running, anyway? We're leaving tracks even Little Red Riding Hood could follow."

"He's right, Ravensmith. We're not even trying to cover our trail."

Eric squatted next to Paige and Steve quickly sat on her other side, giving Eric a possessive sneer. Eric sighed. "We're leaving the trail so they *will* have something to follow. We've been leading them away from the *Columbia* for the past few hours, giving us a little more room to maneuver. By tomorrow, we'll reach the beach and follow it

152

north to where your father's cabin is supposed to be. By the time Fallows reaches the beach, our prints will be washed away and he won't know if we went north or south. There's a good chance he'll split his men up then. That will give us better odds if we have to confront them." He paused. "And it will give me a better chance to get Tim back."

"I understand your feelings about your son, Ravensmith," Paige said. "But we can't help you. We have our own mission to complete. You'll be on your own."

"On my own, huh?" Eric smiled grimly. "That'll be new."

Paige started to say something, changed her mind. It was for the best, anyway. The guy didn't have a chance of getting his son back. He'd probably be killed trying. And that would be convenient all the way around.

Steve picked up a yellow flyer from the ground, began slowly tearing it like a destructive child. "I don't like it, Paige. His plan is too risky. I think we should try to lose them now. Do some backtracking or something. That'll give us a bigger lead."

"We don't want a bigger lead, Captain," Eric explained. "As long as Fallows knows about where we are, he'll keep the pace bearable. Once he thinks we're bolting, he'll come at us full force. I don't think we can outlast seventeen trained troops, do you?"

Steve shrugged, continued tearing paper.

"Well," Eric said, "I think I'll do a little looking

around while you rest. We leave in five minutes."
He ducked into the woods, moving silently away.

"Stop brooding, Steve," Paige said when they were alone. "Ravensmith is right. They push us any harder and we'll be crawling. We may be behind on points, but we're controlling the center of the court."

"What's that supposed to mean?"

"It means that we're goddamn lucky he came along or that maniac Fallows would have killed us all by now."

"Hey, thanks for all the faith."

She shook her head. "Give me a break, Steve. It has nothing to do with you. This Ravensmith character just happens to be better trained than you. Than any of us. He knows what he's doing. Hell, put him on the tennis court and you'd probably slaughter him."

"That supposed to be funny?"

"Christ, grow up." She took a deep breath. "Listen, Steve, we have a mission. Find my father and/or his papers. My dad and I haven't been that close the last few years, but I still want to find him. Bring him home. Family reunion and all that. But we only have another thirty-eight hours. After that the shuttle takes off. I intend to be aboard with or without my father or his papers. A couple of hours in this slime pit has convinced me of that much."

Steve crumbled the paper and tossed it over his shoulder. "OK, I'm just saying I don't think this Ravensmith is as hot as you think. I've had survival training too, you know. I'm saying that we should backtrack now that we've got them going in this direction, circle behind them, and head off in the direction we want. Fallows will just keep going straight ahead, hoping to pick up the trail."

Paige said, "Makes sense."

"Sure it does. The only reason Ravensmith is doing it this way is to split up Fallows's group so he can get his son back. That's his problem, not ours."

"I don't know, Steve." Paige thought about it. Steve sounded so sure of himself. And he was probably right about Ravensmith's motives. Still, she felt a lot more confident with Ravensmith than with Steve. He'd done well so far. "Let's just stick it out a little longer."

"What for?" Steve frowned. "So you can get in his pants?"

"Jesus, Steve."

"I know you, Paige." He wagged his finger accusingly in her face, his own face turning red again. "You're looking for a quick fuck from the tough mountain man. Something different, a little kinky, to tell the folks back in D.C."

"Calm down, Captain!" Paige ordered.

"Fuck you, Doctor." Steve sprang to his feet and stared down at her, his lips twisted into a cruel grin. "I'm doing this my way. I'll get your father or his goddamn secret blueprints or both and meet you back at the shuttle. Then you explain to the boys back home how your pussy got in the way of this mission."

"Captain Connors," Paige said, rising to her

feet. "You are under my command on this mission. I am ordering you to stay here."

Steve chuckled. "Blow it out your ass, wifey." He grabbed his SPAS shotgun and started to leave.

"Steve, goddamn it, stay here."

Capt. Steve Connors spun back and slapped Paige hard across the cheek, knocking her into the tree. "I wanted to do that the whole time we were married. If I'd known how good it felt, I'd have done it long ago." He grinned at her. "That's one thing the ERA ain't never gonna stop. A right cross to the chops." Clutching his shotgun, he jogged off into the woods the same way they'd come.

Eric returned a few minutes later. "Looks clear ahead. No bandits waiting for us that I can see." At first he had assumed that Steve had gone off to take care of bodily functions. But now as Paige turned her face toward him and he saw the red splotch of a hand imprint on her cheek, he knew what had happened. "You OK?"

She nodded. "He'd never hit me before."

"Yeah, well, this island changes people. Even a few hours exposure. Brings out something in people, the things they've managed to hide in civilized society."

She glared at him. "You saying Steve was a latent woman-beater?"

"No, just that you stick someone, anyone, in a savage land, take away all the rules, all the peer pressure, and they're bound to change. Ever drive in your car and have someone cut you off and you

156

wished, right at that moment, you had a gun so you could kill them?"

"Sure, everybody has."

"Only you don't kill them. You think about the morality, the consequences and all that. Besides, you don't usually have a gun in your car. But out here, somebody looks at you funny and you can blow him away, no questions asked."

"That's horrible."

"Yeah, but also kind of freeing. Freedom of choice is heady stuff, especially when no two people are playing by the same rules. You'd better remember that while you're here."

"What rules are you playing by, Ravensmith?"

Eric smiled at her. "Same as you. For now."

Paige said, "Steve intends to beat us to the cabin and then back to the shuttle. He thinks it's some kind of macho game."

"Does he know where the cabin is?"

"Pretty much. I gave him directions as best as I could remember. It's not that hard to find."

"Damn," Eric said, handing her his HK 93. "You hang onto this. I'll move faster without it." He checked the bolt in his bow.

"What are you going to do?"

"I'm going to track down your friend."

"And kill him?"

"Will he come back voluntarily?"

She thought about it a moment. "No."

"Then I'll kill him."

"That's crazy. I won't let you."

"Listen, Doctor. He knows where we're going. What happens if Fallows gets hold of him? He'll know exactly where we're going and why."

"He won't talk."

"Sure he will. I would."

She shook her head. "You don't know Steve."

"You don't know Dirk Fallows. Anybody'd talk. If they were smart, they'd talk before he does anything to them. At least then he might kill you quickly. Otherwise . . ." He shrugged.

"God, sometimes I hate men."

"Me too," Eric said. "We're a pompous bunch all right. But that doesn't change our situation. Captain Connors has got to die." He took a few steps in the direction Steve Connors had gone before he heard the safety flick off.

"You know I'll use this, Ravensmith."

Eric turned, looked into her eyes. Her blond hair was pulled tight into a ponytail. The gun was gripped firmly in both hands. "Yeah." He nodded. "I think you would."

"Then let's push ahead. Steve's got a plan of his own. Maybe he'll make it. He deserves the chance."

"Not when it risks our lives. And my son's."

She patted the metal stock of the HK 93. "You don't really have a choice."

Capt. Steve Connors remembered his jungle survival training well. All the pilots had extensive training back when planes were going down into the Vietnam jungles with the regularity of the sun rising. Three of his pilot buddies were still listed MIA. Right.

Steve had been lucky. A couple close calls, but he never went down. The Connors Charm, they'd called it back then. He'd always been lucky, though. Born into a wealthy family, he'd lettered at prep school in football, basketball, swimming and wrestling. He'd dated the principal's daughter, then at West Point he'd dated General Heinz's daughter, Melanie. Always the best of everything. The Connors Charm.

The only thing he'd wanted he hadn't got was Paige. OK, he had married her for a while. But he'd never really gotten her. She'd always been on her own, living her own life. Maybe even a little stronger than he was at times. Now he wanted her more than ever.

Christ, what had he done back there? Slapped her. She'd never forgive him for that. Never. What had come over him? He'd never hit a woman before, never even came close. But she'd gotten him so angry, ordering him around, flirting with that bastard Ravensmith. He had no choice now. The only way he could redeem himself with her was to find her father or the papers and get them safely back to the shuttle. It was his only hope.

He moved through the woods using the fox walk, just as they'd taught him. His sergeant's Bronx accent rang in his ears now: "Don't none of yous get out dere and walk like yous usually do. Clomp, clomp wit yer heads down and big strides. In da woods you'd scare da animals, sos if da VC ain't hoid ya before, dey hoid yous now. Walk like da fox, short, smooth strides, rolling yer foot from da outside to da inside. Body and head erect, like yer dicks is most of da time."

Steve was pleased as he tramped silently using the fox walk. He'd pause every few hundred yards to listen, but he didn't hear or see any movement. Fallows and his men must be further behind than Ravensmith thought. But just to be safe, he'd start circling soon, covering his tracks. Once Fallows was past him, he could move much faster.

Something came to his mind as he fox walked through the dark forest. A line of poetry of all things. Paige was always trying to get him to read poems and sometimes he'd picked up one of her books just to make her think he actually enjoyed it. He didn't. Still, that line suddenly popped in his head. "The woods are lovely, dark and deep." He didn't remember who wrote it, or what came next. Just one of those things. Maybe when this was all over he'd ask Paige.

Enough backtracking, he thought, and started to veer off into a wide arc. He'd walked less than ten feet from the tracks Eric had left so plainly for Fallows to follow when he heard a rustling in the tree above him. He swiveled the SPAS shotgun up and looked for a target. A man was aiming an M-16 at him. Steve pulled the trigger and the twelve-gauge blew a mushy hole through the man's chest. He dropped from the tree, smacking three or four branches on the way down.

Suddenly, Steve watched the ground open around him as two men who'd been buried in shallow holes and covered with leaves and dead branches popped up with their guns aimed at

160

his head.

One of the men went over to the dead man, prodded him with his boot. Shook his head at his partner.

"Well, well," the partner said, more annoyed than angry. "Get his stuff."

The first gunman stripped the weapons from the dead man.

"What are you going to do?" Steve asked, his voice quivering despite himself.

"That ain't the question, sonny." The second gunman chuckled. "It's what you're gonna do that counts."

"What do you mean?"

"He wants to know what I mean," the first gunman said.

The second gunman grinned. "Let's surprise him."

15.

Col. Dirk Fallows ran his thick calloused hand over his short white hair. The stiff bristles flexed back like the plastic teeth of a comb. "Well, boys, any ideas?"

Cyrus Phelps said, "I think we oughta soak some rawhide in water, see, then tie it real tight around his balls. Then when the sun comes out and dries the rawhide, see, it tightens and crushes his nuts. I read that in a book, I think."

Fallows shook his head. "It's the middle of the night, Phelps. We don't have time to wait for the damned sun to come out."

Phelps shrugged. Hell, he'd tried.

Fallows gazed at Steve Connors, sitting against that big pine tree with his knees huddled against his chest, trying not to look scared and failing miserably. Good, Fallows thought, he's got plenty to be scared about. Listening to a few more lunatic ideas ought to put him in just the right mood. "Anybody else?"

"I don't know, maybe." Dean Leyson stepped forward. He'd served with Fallows in 'Nam. "Remember the time on the Delta, you stripped that guy, some dumb-fuck farmer, and strapped his head to a jigsaw. Then you attached that plastic garbage bag to his butt and dick so that if he had to go to the bathroom, it would go in the bag. Only thing is, you rigged it so any weight in that bag would flip the switch and start the saw. Man, funniest thing I'd ever seen. Thought that gook was gonna explode. Too bad we had to leave early. What do you think happened to him, Colonel?"

Fallows grinned. "What do you think?"

"Yeah." Leyson grinned back. "Yeah."

Someone else, Driscol, said, "We don't got no saw, Leyson, and no electricity. Christ, Colonel, let's just start chopping bits of him off and he'll talk soon enough."

"Right to the point, eh, Driscol?" Fallows said.

"Hell, every minute we fart around here they're getting further away." Suddenly fearing he may have said too much, he quickly added, "Sir."

Fallows reached over, snared Tim around the shoulders, and pulled him forward. "What do you think, Tim? What should we do to make this man talk?"

Tim looked around. Dozens of hard, cruel eyes stared at him, waiting. And then the sad eyes of that man by the tree. "I don't know."

"Come on, Tim. This man knows where your father is. Now that we're sure he's alive, don't you want to know where he is?"

Tim shrugged. "No."

"I see you're still not cured. Still not convinced of where your loyalties belong."

"If what you've told me is correct," Tim said, "and my father has abandoned me, then why would I want to find him?"

"Vengeance, son. It's what makes the world go 'round."

"I see no profit in that. All it can get us is more dead men. For what?"

Fallows smiled. The son of a bitch was learning fast. Fallows didn't dare look at his men because he knew what they were thinking. That the kid was right. Where's the profit? Was what they were going after worth risking their lives? These men needed a carrot dangling before they'd get up in the morning. If someone dared take a vote right now for leader, Fallows suspected the kid might just be a candidate. Too much of his father in him, even at thirteen.

"You're absolutely right, Tim. Vengeance doesn't feed a hungry stomach. What was it Brecht said? 'First eat, and then tell right from wrong.'"

"No," Tim said. "It goes, 'First feed the face, and then tell right from wrong.' From *The Threepenny Opera*."

A couple of men chuckled and Fallows whipped around to look at them. The chuckling stopped. He glared at Tim with such intensity that the boy looked like he wanted to back away. But he didn't. He stared into Fallows's pale eyes without flinching. His father's son, all right. Fallows composed himself, forced a smile. "Well, it's nice to know Eric taught you something. Meantime, we need to find out why your father hooked up with this bozo, and what it has to do with that plane we saw. That's when we discover the profit." He turned to Steve Connors. "I need to know three things from you." He counted off on his fingers. "One, where's Ravensmith? Two, where's the plane? And three, what's your mission?"

Steve Connors peered over his knees at the men surrounding him. Especially at Fallows. Even in the dark, Fallows's eyes were so pale it almost looked like he had no pupils, just white slits like some movie alien.

Steve hugged his knees to keep warm. He knew he was dead meat. No way was this bunch going to let him walk. The only question he had now was how would he act. Would he spill everything and beg for mercy? Would he bawl like a baby, snot running down his nose, blabbering incoherently? Or would he have the guts to spit in their faces and take what they dished out without talking? It was the topic of many heated debates with other pilots, what they would do if they were shot down and captured. Some admitted they'd talk right away. Some said they wouldn't talk no matter what. Steve Connors had never been sure.

Fallows nodded at the two men next to

Connors. They each reached down, grabbed an arm, and yanked him roughly to his feet, bouncing him against the tree. Steve smelled fresh pine sap. It reminded him of Paige's disinfected bathrooms. He smiled at the thought.

Fallows shot a hand forward and clamped his fingers on Steve's throat. "You killed one of my men just now, you stupid son of a bitch." Fallows looked around. "Hey, where's Jackson's body?"

"Still out there," Phelps said.

"Well get out there and bury it, damn it. We don't want every stray wolf and wild dog in the area coming around here tonight. Use your heads."

Phelps slapped Leyson on the arm and the two of them jogged off into the woods after Jackson's body.

Fallows returned his gaze to Steve. "Well, asshole?"

Steve felt his knees shaking. They really do shake when you're scared, he thought. So what are you going to do, Steve Connors, ace pilot?

Fallows's fingers dug around the jugular as if it were faulty wiring he was about to rip out. "I'm listening. Three questions, three answers."

"Ravensmith," Steve croaked.

Fallows smiled, released the grip.

Steve swallowed. The saliva seemed to take forever to slide down his sore throat. He looked at Tim. "Your father swore he'd free you, son. Told me to tell you to just hang on a little—"

Fallows's fist sank into Steve's stomach. "Cuff him," Fallows said.

Steve was still doubled over when he felt his hands being jerked behind him, wrapped around the tree trunk. Metal handcuffs were slapped onto his wrists. He sagged forward trying to catch his breath, the cuffs holding him upright. He'd been hit in the stomach before, but not like that.

"OK, hero, you've had your moment of glory. Now get ready to pay the price." Fallows slowly pulled his knife from its sheath. In the dark, the blade looked black, evil. He tapped it against the side of Steve's neck. "Where's Ravensmith?"

Steve was silent.

Fallows pressed the point into the neck and twisted, gouging out a small hunk of flesh. Steve winced, pulling away. Fallows slipped the blade under Steve's right ear. His voice was quiet, almost a whisper. "Where's Ravensmith?"

Steve's lips quivered, actually ached to speak, but he clamped them shut.

Fallows flicked his wrist and lopped off Steve's ear lobe. The lobe flew a few feet and struck one of Fallows's men in the chest.

"Hey," the man said, brushing the blot of blood on his shirt.

"Sorry, Randall," Fallows said. He laid the cool blade under Steve's other ear. *"Ravensmith."*

A rustling behind them? Phelps and Leyson jogging back into camp.

"He's gone," Phelps panted.

"What?"

"Jackson's gone," Leyson echoed. "Looked all over, but he's just gone."

"All of him?" Fallows asked.

"Clothes and everything."

Fallows frowned. "Probably got dragged away by some wild dogs. Tell the guards to keep an eye out for animals prowling near the camp."

"Right," Phelps said, hurrying off.

Fallows stepped closer to Steve, his face barely two inches from the other man's. "I don't have time to fuck with you anymore. You talk or you suffer. I mean *suffer*."

Steve's voice trembled. He wanted to say more, but all he could manage was, "No talk."

Fallows sighed. "I don't have time for this." Suddenly he thrust his thumb into Steve's left eye, digging deep with the nail, forcing it harder as the thumb slipped under the eyeball. He pried his thumb upward, crushing the pulp of the eye against the hard bone of the socket.

Steve Connors screamed, twisting and bucking against the cuffs as they scraped the skin from his wrists. His smashed eye burned and even though it was medically impossible for him to see with it he swore he saw flames, red flames leaping from the socket. Then with a great sob of agony he sagged into unconsciousness.

Fallows looked around at his men, pleased at the fear in their faces. He pointed his bloody thumb at Leyson. "Throw some water in his face and bring him around. He'll talk now."

Fallows awoke the next day feeling pretty happy. He glanced over at Tim, still cuffed in the sleeping bag next to his. The kid had gotten used

168

to sleeping with his hands behind his back. Giving him a gun and a bullet to hold during the day was one thing, but night was something else.

Capt. Steve Connors had finally talked. Fallows had never met a man who wouldn't under the right circumstances. Finding the right circumstances, that was the trick. With some it was pain, mutilation. With most men it was fear of losing their balls or penis. With women, it was facial disfigurement. Children were the toughest. When they wanted to be stubborn, they could withstand more pain than even the toughest men. Yeah, with kids you had to work on their minds. Confuse them.

The sun had lit the Long Beach Halo like a giant orange fuse. Beautiful day, Fallows thought, checking the clip in his Walther as he did every night before going to sleep and every morning when waking up. He'd thought about everything Connors had told him last night. About the *Columbia*. About Dr. Paige Lyons and her father's work. About where the cabin was. Where Ravensmith was heading.

He couldn't help but smile. It was such an easy plan. Grab the father or the papers, whichever they could find, kill Ravensmith, and force the survivors to fly him back to the mainland. With Tim. With the papers as ransom, the government wasn't about to do anything to him. He'd promised his men that they would all go back, but of course that wouldn't do. He'd have to get rid of them after they captured the craft. But that shouldn't be too hard. Send them out on a phony

169

mission. Or kill them. Whatever.

Meantime, they had to get moving. Now that they knew exactly where Eric and the woman were heading, it wouldn't be long before they caught up.

The men were stirring, scratching, coughing, hacking, spitting. Morning sounds.

"Jesus!" Eli Palmer shouted across the camp. Palmer had been a cop with the LAPD for eight years and wasn't given to sudden exclamations.

"What's the matter, Eli?" someone growled in annoyance.

But Fallows recognized the tone of horror in Eli's voice and was scrambling to his feet with his Walther ready.

Palmer stumbled with uncharacteristic clumsiness toward Fallows. He was pointing backwards in the direction of the tree where they'd left Connors cuffed. Fallows hadn't killed him on the chance the pilot might have more to say this morning.

"Gone," Eli Palmer said, holding up his unbuttoned pants with one hand. "I went over there to take a dump. Son of a bitch is gone."

"Who?" Fallows asked.

"That pilot. Connors."

Fallows was incredulous. "He escaped?"

"No, sir, not exactly."

"What are you saying? Did he spring the cuffs? Did someone saw through them? What?"

Eli Palmer shook his head.

Fallows brushed him aside and marched through the camp. His men fell in behind him as

170

they headed outside camp toward the tree.

When they reached the tree, everyone just stared for a minute. Even Fallows.

Steve Connors was gone. But the cuffs were lying on the ground, still locked. And next to the cuffs were Steve Connors's severed hands, the fingers clenched against great pain.

"Weren't no wild animal," Palmer said, shaking his head. "Them hands were cut off."

16.

Paige pointed to the battered Chevy pickup truck parked in the ditch on the side of the road. The front left tire was flat. A spare was lying next to the flat, the jack lying on top of the spare. The spare was also flat. The bed of the pickup was clean except for some empty cardboard boxes and scraps of cloth. Paige said, "My father's truck."

"Been there awhile," Eric said, indicating some fresh grass that had grown in the skid ruts in the dirt.

They approached the truck cautiously.

Paige peeked through the driver's window as she pulled open the door. She gasped, though there was nothing inside. "Christ," she sighed, shaking her head.

Eric hopped down from the truck bed. "What'd you expect to find?"

"I dunno. A body, I guess, like in those spooky movies. Somebody's always opening a door and a body's always falling out on them."

"Any sign of your father?"

"Like what? A coded note addressed to me pinned to the dash?"

"Take it easy, Doctor."

"Yeah, right," Paige said, climbing into the truck. "And quit calling me Doctor. You don't know what it's like to be called Doctor all the time. Even your friends introduce you as Doctor so-and-so, and everyone goes ohhh, like they expect you to solve their problems. I mean, people still ask me for medical advice. I tell them my doctorate's in physics and they say that's all right, do your best. Shit, you don't know."

"Sure I do," Eric said. "Meet Dr. Ravensmith, Ph.D., history. Also frequent dispenser of medical advice. Everything from cold sores to hemorrhoids. Mrs. Dietrich down the street stopped talking to me when I refused to prescribe Valium for her."

Paige looked directly at him. "History, huh?" She looked away quickly, a little embarrassed. During the past few hours traveling with Ravensmith, she'd been figuring him out, categorizing him. He didn't talk much, but when he did, he knew what he was talking about. He also knew how to move them quickly through the back roads and underbrush. They hadn't run into any other people, which meant that the flyers had worked in scaring off most of the area's inhabitants. But not Ravensmith. She stole another glance at him as he crouched down to look under the truck. He was handsome all right, even with that weird scar along his jaw and neck. He had a prime cut body, too. Not beefy like Steve's, a leaner, wilder musculature. Steve's looked like his had been developed in a gym; Ravensmith's looked like he'd gotten his chasing down coyotes. Still, she'd managed to dismiss him as just another ex-military type, cocky and bullying. Except for his single-minded drive to recover his son. That touched her. Now she finds he's got a goddamn history doctorate. Bastard wasn't easy to pigeonhole.

"History, huh?" she repeated.

"Yeah."

"Professor?"

"Assistant professor." He smiled. "But with tenure."

She stared into his eyes, noticing for the first time how penetrating they were. Even when he was smiling at you, he was searching, probing.

"So, Dr. Lyons," he said. "What shall I call you?"

"Try Lyons."

"How about Paige?"

She shrugged, flipped open the glove compartment. "Sure, OK. Whatever."

"Move over." Eric nudged her.

She gave him an annoyed look but scooted across the dirty seat while pawing through the mess of papers and used tissues that stuffed the glove compartment. "Dad hasn't changed. Still a slob."

Eric noticed the warm affection under the chiding tone, filed that away. Something to use later. He knew she had no intention of taking Tim back on the *Columbia*, that she was just using him. But he'd find a way. First, though, he had to find her father. And Tim.

"My God, I don't believe it," she said, reaching deep into the glove compartment. Crushed styrofoam cups spilled onto the floor. When Paige's hand reappeared, it was wrapped around a full can of Coke. "He used to drink at least a six-pack of these every day. We'd all sit around the breakfast table drinking orange juice and he'd be guzzling a can of Coke." She smiled fondly at the memory. "Told us if it weren't for cola he'd have been an alcoholic."

Eric looked at the can, felt his taste buds contract. He hadn't had a soft drink or a beer in months. Finding fresh water had been enough of a chore. "You going to drink that?" he asked softly.

"Are you kidding. It's warm."

Eric took it from her and carefully eased the pop-top open. He didn't want to do it too fast and have it all fizz out. He wanted every last drop. The top hissed, sprayed some warm cola onto his pants and across his hands. He licked his hands while waiting for the foam to die down. He leaned his head back on the seat and drank half the can in one swig. "Jesus, that's good."

She gave him a disgusted look. "Just don't

belch, OK? I hate that."

He drank the rest of the Coke. Belched. "Couldn't be helped," he said.

Paige ignored him, continued rummaging through the glove compartment. "Nothing here. Mostly trash. Credit card receipts for gas, grocery lists, deck of cards, a Doonesbury cartoon book. Some tape cassettes of Judy Collins."

"No top secret documents to save the world?"

"Half a pack of Juicy Fruit. You interested?"

"Stale?"

"What's the difference? I'm surprised you didn't rip open the Coke can and lick the insides."

Eric said, "You haven't been here long enough to pass judgment on my manners, lady."

Paige flushed, her cheeks glowing red. She jumped out of the passenger side and slammed the truck door hard. The truck rocked. She marched all the way around the truck before standing in front of Eric, her face still a bit pink. She was breathing hard, her mouth a tight slit. Then she took a deep breath and closed her eyes. When she opened them again, it was as if a different person was staring out. "I'm sorry, Eric. I mean it. I know how I act sometimes, I mean I can see me making a fool of myself. Inside I cringe, but that only makes me charge ahead even harder. You're right, I tend to pass out judgments on people like I was sent directly from God. I don't mean anything by it. Really."

Eric said, "Does that mean I get the Juicy Fruit?"

She laughed. "Ladies first." She unwrapped one stale piece, shoved it in her mouth and began chewing. She tossed the rest of the pack to Eric. "Help yourself. Only I suggest kneading it with your tongue before chewing. Save your teeth."

Eric stepped out of the truck and looked around. "How far to the cabin?"

"Another couple miles. Three at most."

"Then the truck was coming from the cabin, not going toward it."

"Looks that way."

"It also looks like he had the truck loaded with some of his stuff. Got a flat tire here, but when he took out the spare, he found that was flat too."

"Typical of him to have a flat spare."

"Absent-minded professor, huh?"

"No, not really. Just didn't care much about the details of daily living. He didn't forget things, he just ignored them."

"Like his daughter?"

"No!" she snapped, the anger back. Then it was gone, under control. "No. Actually we were very close until I got into the astronaut program. Then we didn't see much of each other. Not his fault. He called every Monday, invited me to fly out just about twice a month, planned dinners with me whenever he was in D.C." Paige sighed. "I was the one who drifted away. So busy trying to make it on my own, proving I wasn't just the famous Dr. Lyons's daughter, that I, well, pushed us apart, I guess."

"When's the last time you saw him?"

"Over a year before the quakes. A year and a half."

"Well, from the looks of things here, whoever was driving this truck probably returned to the cabin. Maybe to look for something to repair the tire."

"Then why didn't they come back? Where did the stuff that was in the back go?"

"I don't know. Maybe he realized there was no place to go anymore. Figured he was safest staying home. Maybe he carried the stuff back or someone else made off with it. No way of knowing until we find the cabin."

"Then let's go."

"Just a second," Eric said, reaching back into the truck's glove compartment and grabbing the two cassette tapes. He stuffed them into his shirt pocket.

"You some kind of Judy Collins fan?"

"Sometimes. Only right now I'm just curious."

"About what?"

"About why he's got the cassette tapes in the truck, but no cassette player."

"That's the cabin," Paige whispered. Only it really wasn't a cabin at all. More like a converted barn. "It looks different."

"You sure this is the place?"

"Yeah, I'm sure. It's just . . . oh, never mind." How could she explain that she remembered it as it was when she'd last seen it, through a sixteen-year-old's romantic eyes. It had been their family retreat, a place to hike and run and yell at the top of your lungs if you wanted. Christ, now it looked old, weather-beaten. Shabby.

She started toward it, trancelike.

Eric touched her shoulder. "Better wait."

"For what?"

"To make sure it's safe."

Paige let the implication register for a moment. "OK."

"Besides, what makes you think he wouldn't have taken off with the others when he read your phony flyers?"

"No way. Not Dad. He'd know the government would have to get him out sooner or later, and he'd certainly recognize this silly ploy as their style."

Eric stared at the house awhile. Nothing unusual about it. Someone had spent a lot of money a long time ago to have this place built. It wasn't a barn, merely built to look like one that had been converted, a popular style years ago. But time and neglect had ravaged its appearance. Yet there was something a little funny. The windows were clean.

"How was your father on housework?"

"A menace. Last time I saw him he told me he'd converted entirely to paper plates and plastic forks rather than wash any dishes."

"Better call in again, see if your friend's made it back."

"Right." Paige pulled the transmitter from her

179

backpack, tapped out a coded message. It wasn't Morse or any of the others Eric knew, so he just watched the house while she and Dr. Bart Piedmont conversed in dots and dashes. It didn't matter anyway; he already knew what the answer would be.

"Well, Steve isn't back yet." She was trying to sound casual, but Eric could hear the tightness in her voice. "Guess he's slower than we thought."

"Might have sprained an ankle or something."

"Yeah, right." Paige began chewing on her thumbnail, a habit she'd been fighting for the past fifteen years. "Could have sprained an ankle, or gotten a little lost."

"Uh-huh."

"But you don't believe that?"

"I don't know. But just in case, we'd better start working fast, OK?"

She nodded. "OK."

"Let's go. Keep three feet behind me and to the left. If anything spooks me, I'm diving to the right. You drop where you are and get ready to shoot. Clear?"

"Clear."

They both lifted their HK 93s, checked the clips and flipped the safeties off. Eric's crossbow was slung over his shoulder.

"Just don't accidentally shoot my father, OK?" She wasn't being smart, it was a sincere plea.

"As long as he doesn't shoot at us."

"He's never even fired a gun in his whole life."

"Lucky man. Only since the quakes, a lot of

people have done a lot of things they'd never done before, or ever thought they could do." He pointed his gun at the front of the house. "Like I said, people have changed, but most haven't gotten neater. You say your dad was a slob, but those windows are spotless. That's unusual out here. Most people are too busy surviving to do anything more than the minimum of cleaning."

"You've made your point, Eric. Let's get on with it."

Eric lead the way through the thick weeds and thorny underbrush. Paige gripped her HK 93 tightly, her teeth clenched so hard her jaw ached.

The thirty yards around the house were cleared. What weeds and grass grew there had been pulled or tramped down. Eric stopped when he reached the edge of this yard. He tensed his finger around the trigger with one hand and cupped the other around his mouth. "Hey!" he shouted at the house. "Dr. Lyons?"

There was no answer. He could see no one at the windows either.

"Anybody in there? We're not looking for any trouble."

Paige waded forward a few steps and shouted, "Daddy! It's Paige."

No answer.

"Now what?" Paige said, more to herself than Eric. Her voice was heavy with disappointment. She let the HK 93 sag to her side.

"Maybe he's being cautious."

"Sure," she said. "And maybe he's dead."

"Maybe. But as I understand your mission, you're to bring back either your dad or his papers. Right?"

"Yes."

"Then we go ahead. If he's not in there, maybe there's some sign of where he went."

"Like a body."

"Like a map, a letter."

"A treasure map?" She scowled at him. "You think I'm only here for his lousy plans, don't you? Little Paige, government robot who follows orders no matter what. Maybe that's how you were, mister, when you were in 'Nam, but I'm not built that way. Yes, I want his papers, but I want him more."

Eric touched her shoulder. "I didn't doubt that, Paige. I didn't mean a treasure map, but something to indicate where he might have gone. You said he was expecting to be rescued."

"Yes." She brightened. "Yes, he might have done something like that. He was very meticulous when it came to his work."

"Well, let's find out." He started toward the house, crouching low, the gun set on semiautomatic.

A movement behind the window, someone peeking and ducking away. Too fast for Eric to see a face clearly. "Someone's home," he whispered over his shoulder.

"Let's huff and puff and blow the house down."

Eric patted his HK 93. "That's what these are for."

They were only fifteen yards away now, Paige

still behind and to the left of Eric. She was chewing on a sliver of thumbnail that had come off earlier.

"Come on out," Eric said to the front door. "We don't mean you any harm."

The front door flew open and they all came charging out at once.

17.

"Five minutes," Fallows told his men. "That's all."

The men stopped running, some holding their sides, trying to rub out the stitches that had settled into their muscles a mile or so back. Others just dropped to the ground, panting and puffing, fumbling open their canteens, guzzling water. Bedlow was hugging a tree, vomiting on the bark. But no one complained. It was hard to while being watched by Fallows, who wasn't even breathing hard.

"You all on your periods?" Fallows laughed, brushing his white hair with his hand. "Christ, even this little kid can outrun you sissies."

Tim stood next to Fallows, fighting to control his breathing. He wanted nothing more than to drop to the ground with the others and gulp air like a dying fish, but he wouldn't give them the satisfaction. He regulated his breathing, just as his father had taught him. Besides, Fallows pointing him out like that made him feel kind of proud. Funny, he never thought he'd feel that around here. He shoved his hand in his pocket, felt the smooth casing of the 9mm bullet.

"Soon, kid," Fallows said, patting Tim's shoulder, "I'm going to have your father right where I had him in 'Nam. Then you're going to see what he's really made of. The kind of man who let his family be destroyed that way. Who abandoned them the way he abandoned me. He could've been my partner, made a fortune with me. Wars are God's way of letting the strong get rich. But he turned me in instead. Testified against me. Well, he's done the same to you, Tim. That's why we have to stick together."

Tim wanted to cry out, defend his father, but he was afraid Fallows would take his bullet away. And he wanted that bullet more than anything in the world. Besides, Fallows wasn't saying anthing that Tim hadn't sometimes thought himself. Why hadn't his father rescued him yet? Was he even going to try? If he was, what was he doing up here where Fallows had to chase him?

Eli Palmer was running down the road toward them, his heavy boots thumping the dirt road. "Sir . . . sir . . ." he panted.

"Speak, Palmer," Fallows said impatiently.

"Up ahead . . . abandoned truck. Same as that pilot said . . . belonged to the . . . scientist."

"Any sign of the man?"

"No, sir. Truck had a flat, so'd the spare. No sign of foul play."

Foul play. Christ, Fallows thought, once a cop always a cop. "What about papers? Anything?"

"No. Nothing. But looks like someone has already rummaged through the glove compartment. Probably recently."

Fallows could see by Eli's expression that he was waiting to be asked. Fucking cops. "How do you figure that, Eli?"

"Well, the truck had been there quite awhile. Weeks at least. But I found an empty Coke can in the cab and there were still a few sticky drops on it." Eli Palmer smiled, having finally proved that he had belonged in Homicide rather than Burglary, just what he'd been telling the department for three years before the quakes.

"Good work, Eli." Fallows smiled. "They can't be too far away. We take it slow and easy from now on. I don't want to spook him. Let's go."

Everyone was on their feet and following Fallows.

Fallows turned to Tim and grinned. "Still got that bullet, kid?"

"Yes."

"Good. You're going to need it."

18.

There were maybe twenty of them. They ran out of the house, circling Paige and Eric like Indians attacking a wagon train. Only they didn't attack. They stood still, each holding something to use as a weapon. A hammer, a saw, a hunk of firewood, a screwdriver, a fork.

The oldest was a girl of about fifteen. She wore a tattered but clean dress and a full-length apron. Her blond hair hung down her back almost to her waist. The weapon she was brandishing was a wooden spatula.

The rest of the children stood silently, obviously waiting for her command. The youngest was about three. He carried a sharp stick that reminded Eric of roasting hot dogs.

"Hi," the oldest girl said. Her voice was neutral,

187

her eyes wary. She gripped the spatula tightly as she studied Paige's and Eric's automatic weapons.

"Hi," Paige replied. "We don't mean you any harm."

The girl waved the spatula at the guns. "Then put those things down."

"Can't do that," Eric said. "We're being followed by some men who want to kill us."

The girl shrugged. It wasn't her problem. "Then maybe you should go."

"What's your name?" Paige asked her. "My name's Paige."

One of the young boys giggled. "Page? Like in a book?"

"Yes," Paige said.

Several of the children giggled.

"I'm Wendy," the girl said. "What do you want?"

"We're looking for a man, an older man in his sixties. About my height, gray hair and a thick moustache. He used to live here."

Wendy shook her head. "No adults live here. Just us kids."

"No adults?"

"That's right."

Eric could see Paige trying not to show her disappointment, but her shoulders sagged and her eyes were shining with held-back tears. He stepped toward Wendy and all the other children lifted their weapons and stepped toward him. He looked at them and stopped. "May we come inside and look around? The man we're looking for used to live here. Maybe he left something behind to tell us where he's gone."

"There's lots of stuff inside. We just left most of it."

Paige brightened. "May we look?"

Wendy hesitated, studying their faces with a child's skeptical eye. She looked at the guns again and sighed as if she had no choice. "I guess. Only don't mess things up, OK? We've been cleaning all morning. Peter will be back soon."

"Peter?" Eric said.

"Yeah. He's out hunting. Me and Peter take care of everyone. Kinda like their parents, see."

"What happened to everybody's real parents?"

"I dunno. Dead. I guess. Peter and I were on a field trip with some other students from Uni High in L.A. We were studying tide pools for Mrs. Levy's biology class. Then the quakes hit and most everybody else in the class was killed. Mrs. Levy fell into the ocean and got pulled out to sea. Me and Peter started running. We passed this junior high school and tried to steal a couple bikes so we could get away faster. The whole building had collapsed. Dead kids and teachers everywhere. We grab the bikes and start pedaling out of there when we see some kids wandering around bawling. They'd been on the playground of some elementary school when it hit. With everybody around us dead, they started following me and Peter. We finally ended up here."

"Was it empty when you got here?"

"Sure. Otherwise we wouldn't have stayed, right? The place was a mess, I can tell you that. It's bad enough picking up after all these kids, but when the place was so gross to start . . . Well, I guess we can't complain. At least we have a home now."

Eric and Paige exchanged looks.

"So you and Peter have been taking care of all these kids by yourselves?" Eric asked.

"We ain't babies," one of the boys snapped. He was about eleven.

"We do our share," one of the girls, ten, added.

There was some muttered approval among the others.

"All rights, that's enough," Wendy scolded gently. "Let's wash those grimy little paws and get ready for lunch. I haven't been slaving over a hot fire all day for nothing, right?"

The kids scattered to behind the house.

"Got a pump back there," Wendy explained. "Whoever was here before rigged it up. We get all the water we need. I guess that's why we never left. Here at least we can eat and drink."

Eric nodded, looked around. "And you're pretty isolated, too. Ever bothered by strangers?"

"Up here?" She laughed. "Nope. Oh, once some couple and their kid wandered by, wanted to stay and take over from me and Pete. But the kids voted them down and they moved on. Thing is—" she grinned—"their kid wanted to stay with us. They dragged him away crying and screaming."

"Sounds like you've made quite a home here," Eric said.

"We have. Better than some these kids came from. Sure, sometimes we miss our folks, and we've had a few runaways go off looking for their parents. But mostly we just take care of each other." She looked at her watch. "I gotta get back to the cooking now. You wanna come in and look around, fine." She turned and walked back into the house, leaving the door open for Paige and Eric to follow.

"Jesus," Paige said.

"Yeah," Eric said.

They walked into the house.

The inside was consciously rustic. Lots of clumpy wooden furniture and rough wood walls. Even the ceiling was bare beams. Walking into this house gave Eric a funny feeling. Everything was so neat and normal looking, he could almost forget there had been a disaster.

Wendy strolled straight through the living room and dining room out into the kitchen. A little girl with pigtails peeked around the corner at Eric and Paige. She hugged a doll made out of a stuffed sock and button eyes.

"Hi," Eric said.

She smiled, hugged the doll closer.

"What's your name?"

"Sarah," she mumbled into her sock doll.

"What's his name?" Eric pointed at the doll.

"I dunno."

"Come on."

"Rupert, I guess."

Paige was rummaging through the drawers of the oak desk in the corner by the old TV console. The TV screen was dust-free and the rusty rabbit ears still formed a neat V, even though there was no electricity, no TV stations broadcasting. She struggled with one drawer, finally forcing it open. Like the rest of the drawers, it was stuffed with papers. "Hey, Eric, how about giving me a hand here, huh? Play Mr. Charm later."

Sarah frowned at Eric. "Is she your mother?"

Eric laughed.

Paige shook her head disgustedly. "Kids."

Eric winked at Sarah and she giggled and ran into the kitchen. He walked over to Paige and started pulling wads of folded paper from the drawers.

"Wendy must've just shoved everything that Dad had lying on the desk into these drawers. Christ, she may be even a bigger neat freak than I am."

"Is this how you remember the place?"

"Pretty much. Same furniture and everything. It's just cleaner than I've ever seen it. It's like some TV household. Like on *Leave It to Beaver* or *The Donna Reed Show*. Know what I mean?"

Eric nodded.

She glanced around the room fondly. "Still, I guess they're just making the best home they can. Did a hell of a job, I'd say."

Eric unfolded papers with scrawled mathematical equations, handed them to Paige. "This look like anything?"

She looked at them, tossed them on top of the desk. "Doodles. Some of these are scraps of ideas, but not the whole blueprint. Not even enough to make much sense."

Eric walked over to one of the bookshelves that lined an entire wall of the living room. A Sanyo cassette tape recorder held up a row of Britannica encyclopedias. Eric lifted it from the shelf and a couple volumes collapsed. There was a tape already in the machine. Eric pressed Play. Nothing happened.

"Batteries are dead," Wendy said from the doorway. "They weren't when we got here, but one of the kids played some Peter, Paul and Mary tape that was in there and left it on overnight. We couldn't find any more batteries."

Sarah stood behind Wendy, still hugging the sock doll to her throat. "I didn't mean to do it," she whined.

"Never mind, Sarah," Wendy said. "It doesn't matter. We can still sing same as always. Don't need batteries for that." She pointed at the ancient upright piano in the dining room.

"You play?" Eric asked.

"I'm teaching myself. When there's time." She smiled proudly. "Meantime, I read stories to the children at night from those books." She pointed to a stack next to the worn easy chair. The top one was *Peter Pan*.

"Oh," Eric said. Of course. Peter and Wendy. "What's your real name, Wendy?"

The girl who called herself Wendy smiled. "Grace Yedonski. Ugh. I like Wendy better."

"What about Peter?"

"Louis Southern. But don't call him anything but Peter, OK? Makes him mad."

"OK."

"Look," Wendy said, "I'd appreciate it if you'd hurry up and find what you came for. Peter will be

193

back soon and he doesn't like strangers. Gets the kids all stirred up."

"Must be hard on you," Paige said, "taking care of so many children."

Wendy shrugged. "It's not bad. They need me."

"We're almost done, Wendy," Eric said. "A few more minutes. OK?"

She hesitated, nibbled her bottom lip, then nodded. "OK. But hurry." She went back to the kitchen, Sarah trotting behind her.

"You might think this is funny," Paige said, staring after Wendy, "but I kind of admire her. The way she and this Peter kid take care of all these children."

"They seem to really care," Eric agreed.

"Yeah, well, while she is scrubbing and cooking and keeping these kids alive, it's time for us more mature adults to get back to the really important task of finding some stupid papers."

Eric pointed at her backpack. "Got any batteries in there?"

"In my flashlight, sure."

"Hand 'em over."

"They won't fit that thing."

"They will when I'm done." Eric pulled some wires from the back of the stereo and adjusted them to the small recorder. Within a few minutes he had the Sanyo working. He popped in one of the Judy Collins tapes. Judy Collins sang "Both Sides Now."

"So much for that theory, eh, master spy?" Paige said.

Eric punched the Fast Forward button, then

Play. Judy Collins singing "Send in the Clowns." He repeated this several times. Finally he got something else. Obviously a home taping of someone playing the piano, clumsily picking out single notes.

Paige stopped fussing with the papers in the desk and listened.

"Your dad know how to play the piano?"

"The way you and I breathe. That can't be him. The notes don't make any musical sense, they sound like random plunking."

"Code, maybe. Notes corresponding with letters and numbers."

"Of course!"

Eric ejected the tape. "He must've figured someone would come for him, but he probably couldn't be sure. So he put it all in code on these tapes."

"But where is he? He wouldn't have just left them in the truck."

"He might have. Maybe he came back here for something to fix the flat, but when he got back to the truck, someone was unloading it. They might've been armed and he didn't want to risk getting shot by looters, so he ran. The tapes sure weren't worth his life, especially when he could always make more."

Paige sat on the edge of the desk. "Yeah, that's possible. Otherwise, he would have left some sign, some way for us to find him."

Eric looked at his watch. "There's not enough time for us to look for him right now. We'll have to take the tapes back. Maybe there's something

195

on them about where he was heading. They can always send someone back after him."

Paige stared at him. "You know better. Once they have this, that's the end of it."

The front door swung open with a thud and a tall, skinny boy of sixteen strode in with a scowl on his face. "What's going on? Who are you?" He pulled a rust-pocked machete from his belt.

"Hold on," Eric said, raising his hands. "Peter, right?"

Wendy came bustling out from the kitchen, Sarah in tow. "It's all right, Peter. They don't want to hurt us."

Peter didn't look like he was buying that as he walked slowly toward Eric, interested not in the HK 93, but in the crossbow slung over Eric's back.

"Neat," he said, for a moment reverting back to his own age. But when he looked at Wendy the burden of responsibility crowded aside his youthful features and he was scowling again, brandishing his machete. "What do you want?"

"This house used to belong to my father—"

"Well, we live here now," Peter said. "And we ain't leaving."

"I don't want you to," Paige continued. "We were just looking for something that might tell us where he's gone." Paige described him. "Have you seen him?"

Peter thought about it for a while. "Moustache, huh? Saw this body over near the ravine, had a moustache. He was old, had some gray."

Paige looked pained. "What about his eyes?

What color?"

Peter shrugged. "Dunno. He didn't have no eyes anymore. Birds got to 'em, I guess." He made a pecking motion with his fingers.

Paige lunged another step toward him and he reflexively lifted the machete at her. "How old was he?"

"Old. Maybe forty."

Paige sighed. "Christ. Kids."

"We're not fucking kids, lady," Peter exploded. "We're a family. You got the fancy weapons, so if you're gonna use 'em, go ahead. Otherwise, get your asses outta here."

"Language, Peter," Wendy clucked.

Eric looked at Paige. "Let's go."

"Not yet. Look, Peter, I'm sorry. You and Wendy have done a terrific job here. I mean that."

Peter accepted the compliment with the same proud expression that Wendy had shown earlier. "We done all right."

"So let us stay a few minutes longer. Let me try to work out some of the message on these tapes with your piano." She looked at Eric. "Maybe there's something on here about where he was going."

Eric looked at his watch.

"It's probably a very simple code, Eric," she pleaded. "Just give me half an hour."

Eric gestured at Peter. "It's your house, man. What do you say?"

Peter and Wendy exchanged glances, little smiles. It was the same kind of silent exchanges Eric and Annie used to have. That secret language of lovers.

"Half an hour," Peter agreed. "In exchange for that fancy bow."

Eric started to shake his head, saw the desperate look in Paige's eyes, and sighed. "OK."

Peter clapped his hands together and rubbed them happily. "Right. Why don't we let your lady alone in here while we go outside and you show me how to shoot that thing."

Eric stroked his scar, his mouth grim. Sure, he had the HK 93 now, but he'd had the crossbow since the quakes. It had saved his life several times. He didn't like parting with it.

Paige carried the cassette player to the piano, lifted the lid, and turned back to Eric. When she spoke, her voice was husky with emotion. "Thanks, Eric."

Eric tossed the two cassettes to her and followed Peter out the door.

Paige sat at the piano, listening to the tape, matching the notes on the piano, scribbling them down on paper. She broke the code immediately. It was simple, just as she'd thought. Each letter of the alphabet corresponded to a note on the piano. She had a couple sentences written when she heard a noise behind her. Startled, she turned around.

"Hi," Sarah said, cradling her sock doll, Rupert.

"Hi, Sarah." Paige smiled, turning back to her work. Cute kid, she thought, then was lost again in the code, forgetting Sarah was even there.

Sarah took tiny steps toward Paige. When she

was only a foot behind her, Sarah reached inside her sock doll and pulled out a corroded pipe wrench. Some of the stuffing came out with the wrench. She picked clumps of stuffing from the wrench and carefully tucked them back into her sock doll. When that was done, she lifted the wrench over her head with both hands and brought it down on the back of Paige's head.

Wendy stepped out from the kitchen, wiping her hands on her apron. She looked at Paige lying on the floor and at Sarah standing there with the bloody wrench. She smiled at Sarah. "Good girl, Sarah. Good girl."

19.

"So how does that thing work?" Peter said.

Eric laid his HK 93 on the ground. Then he unslung the crossbow and held it out for Peter to examine. "You ever own a BB gun?"

"Nah. My parents wouldn't let me. But Aaron Roth down the street used to let me use his sometimes. We'd shoot Coke cans in his back yard."

"Well, this bow cocks just like a lot of BB guns, only it takes a lot more strength, so you usually put it on the ground and lean into it. Like this." Eric pushed the nose of the bow against the ground, leaned his body into it, and the cocking mechanism slid back until the bowstring was pulled back into the trigger. He straightened up and handed the bow to Peter. The weight surprised Peter, for the bow dropped a few inches in his hands.

"Jeez, this sucker's heavy." He hefted it a few times, grinning.

Eric smiled at the boy's delight. It had been a long time since he'd played teacher. He could imagine his classroom now back at the university, the students laughing at something, or arguing with him about some point, or groaning as he explained their next assignment. It was a role that had suited him well. Much more than his previous one of commando or his present one of avenger. From the house, the single notes from the piano echoed crisply in the warm air. He would give Paige a few more minutes tinkering with the code. Then they would have to leave. He still had to hunt down Fallows and steal Tim. Steal him? Funny word to choose, as if he were taking something that belonged to someone else. But that was his fear, wasn't it? That Fallows, with all the time he'd had with Tim, had somehow brainwashed him. He'd done it before in less time. Almost had done it to Eric.

"Whoosh," Peter said, aiming down the length of the empty crossbow. "Thud. Got him."

"Just be sure you don't fire a bow without an arrow. Damages the bow." He looked at his watch. Twenty-three hours left to retrieve Tim and get back to the shuttle. Less than a day.

The piano notes had stopped coming from the house. Good, maybe she was done. He'd show

Peter how to shoot the bow then they could be on their way.

A few kids drifted from around the back of the house, wandering toward Eric and Peter. Eric noticed that little Sarah was among them. Together they formed a little group of eight curious onlookers, silently watching. Most of them looked pretty healthy and clean, but a couple of them looked a bit pale and sickly. Well, that was to be expected under the circumstances. No medical supplies up here. No doctor. They were lucky to have food and water and shelter.

"Can I try it with an arrow?" Peter asked.

"Let me show you how first," Eric said. He took the bow back, slid a bolt into the brass groove. "Like this, see? With the guide feather in the groove."

"Yeah."

Eric twisted away from Peter, thumbed the safety button, and swung around again with the bow against his shoulder. "That branch," he said, indicating a gnarled stick of wood the size of a baseball bat about fifty feet away. He squeezed the trigger. The bolt rocketed from the bow with a whiz and dove straight into the stick, chipping off a chunk of wood.

"Wow," Peter said, impressed.

The group of children behind them applauded. They started to walk closer.

Eric turned and smiled at them. "Hi, kids."

They smiled back but didn't answer.

Eric winked at Sarah. "Hi, Sarah."

She hugged her sock doll to her neck and giggled. "Hi, mister."

The children all walked closer.

"Careful now," Eric warned. "Don't get too close to that gun. It's dangerous."

The children smiled, but kept walking.

"I mean it now," Eric said sternly.

They stopped. One of the kids started coughing so violently his little baseball cap fell off. Beneath the cap he was almost bald. Eric noticed some hair loss among a couple of the other sickly kids.

"What's wrong with them?" Eric asked Peter.

Peter shrugged. "Cold or flu, I guess. They'll be OK."

"You don't cook indoors do you?"

"Nope. Wendy keeps a fire outside the back door for cooking. She read that burning some kinds of wood inside can be harmful. Sometimes we have a fire inside, but only with dry branches around here. We're pretty careful."

Eric nodded. The kids were pretty smart.

"Can I try it, Mr. Ravensmith?" Peter begged. "Shoot your bow?"

"Sure, Peter."

He handed Peter the bow and a sharp bolt.

Peter smiled. So did the rest of the children.

They sure are a happy bunch of kids, Eric thought as he watched Peter cock the bow and slide the bolt into place.

"Hurry up, children. Get the shoes first."

Wendy's voice broke through Paige's haze as if it were being carried through a heating duct from one apartment to another. She felt little hands tugging at her shoes. She tried to kick them away.

"Oh fudge!" Wendy said. "She's alive."

Paige struggled to lift her aching head from the floor as her eyes adjusted to the semi-darkness of the small room. All she could make out was a cluster of little faces hovering around her and, above them, Wendy, looking flustered.

"Darn," Wendy said. "I was sure she was dead. Billy, hand me that knife there. No, not that one. The long one with the teeth."

"What are you doing?" Paige asked, lifting herself to her elbows, despite the throbbing at the back of her head. Tiny hands reached out and started pushing her back to the floor. She brushed a few aside, but there were so many of them. And now Wendy was leaning over her with that long, saw-toothed knife.

"I'm sorry, ma'am," Wendy said. "Really sorry. We thought you were already dead."

"Dead?" Paige repeated numbly. Then she remembered the thump on her head. "Sarah."

Wendy nodded. "Yes, usually Sarah's much more reliable. She clobbers someone they're usually down for good. I guess her aim was a little off this time."

"I don't understand. Where am I?"

Wendy smiled slightly. "Used to be the pantry."

Paige's eyes focused slowly on the surroundings. In the dark she hadn't recognized it. Sure, the pantry. How many times had she hid in this room nibbling Fig Newtons until she was sick? But it wasn't as she remembered it. There were objects of all sizes hanging from the ceiling. Beneath each thing was a pan or a bucket. A couple objects were still dripping into their pans. The smell of the room was different too. Heavy. Sickly rich.

Wendy's apron was dark, smeared with something.

Paige swung her arms, knocking three children backwards into a couple hunks of whatever was hanging. One kicked a pan and the dark liquid slapped over the edge and spilled across the wooden floor.

Paige scrambled to her feet, reeling slightly from the pain in her head. A rush of dizziness spun her awkwardly around. She started to swoon, her eyes fluttering shut as she fell, but she caught herself on the edge of a large, metal garbage can. The same battered one that she'd used the lid from as a shield when she and her father had used broom handles to swordfight twenty years ago.

"God," Paige said, trying to catch her breath and balance so she could fight back. She still didn't know what these kids were up to, only that they had tried to kill her. And were going to try again. She felt their little hands grabbing at her arms and she fought the nausea, forcing her eyes wide. As she did, she found herself staring into the gaping mouth of the trash can.

And saw the pile of human bones filling the can. Mixed with the bones were chunks of flesh, strips of human skin.

"Oh no! Oh my God, please!" she gasped, barely able to get enough air to say even that.

"Hold her down!" Wendy ordered and the children began shoving at Paige, trying to tackle her to the ground.

Paige flung the one clinging to her right arm against the trash can. He slammed into it, knocking it over. The contents spilled onto the floor in a clatter of dry bones. But rolling out across the bones came a severed head, hair matted with blood. One eye gouged out, the other wide with terror.

Steve Connors.

As Paige stared at the head, she hardly felt the fists pummeling her stomach and back. Hardly felt herself being dragged to the floor. Hardly felt the children sitting on her arms and legs. Barely noticed Wendy's apologetic shrug as she came toward her with the knife saying, "Sorry, ma'am, but we got a lot of mouths to feed around here."

Eric studied the children as Peter struggled to cock the bow. These kids had something to be proud of. They'd formed a family and survived when a lot of other kids their age had died of starvation or been murdered by scavengers. Too bad about the sick ones, though. The little kid in the baseball cap coughed again, wiped some mucus from his nose with his sleeve.

"Not as easy as it looks, huh?" Eric said to Peter.

"I'll get it," Peter said defiantly.

Eric smiled, looked at his watch. Paige had stopped playing the piano almost five minutes ago, but she still hadn't left the house. Maybe she was chatting with the children, or helping them with something. They certainly were an endearing bunch.

"Got it," Peter announced, finally cocking the bow. He laid the arrow into the brass groove just as Eric had shown him.

"Good," Eric said. "Now aim it at your target, sight right through there, and gently squeeze the trigger. Don't jerk it."

Peter swung the crossbow up and pointed it at Eric's chest. The children applauded. Peter squeezed the trigger.

Nothing happened.

Peter looked startled, then panicky. He squeezed the trigger again, pulling hard. Still, the bow wouldn't fire. "Shoot, damn it, *shoot!*"

Eric reached out and grabbed the crossbow away from Peter, shoving the boy to the ground as he did. "The one thing I didn't show you or tell you, was how to release the safety. I never do that with someone I don't know until I'm sure of his target. Now, you want to explain to me what's going on?"

"Go to hell!" Peter said, still prone on the ground.

207

Eric heard the footsteps pattering behind him and turned in time to catch Sarah's wrist and shake the wrench free from her hand. He pushed her away. "What's the matter with you kids? We don't want to harm you."

Then the kid in the baseball cap began to cough and the truth flashed on Eric. He spun, saw Peter groping for his machete, and fired the arrow into Peter's right thigh. The 175 pounds of tension hammered the bolt through the leg and partially into the ground, pinning Peter there. He howled with pain.

Eric slung the bow over his shoulder and grabbed the HK 93 from the ground. He ran toward the house, the gun set for semiautomatic bursts.

"Hear that?" Fallows said.

"What?" Bedlow asked.

"That yelling. Someone yelling."

Bedlow listened. The rest of the men listened. They all shook their heads. Bedlow said, "I don't hear anything, Colonel."

Fallows looked at Tim. "What about you, kid? You hear anything?"

Tim listened. He didn't so much hear anything as felt it, like a slight vibration, a tremor in the wind that didn't belong. "There's something."

"He's just saying that," Phelps said. "He don't hear shit."

Fallows smiled at Tim. "See what I'm up against?"

There it was again, Tim thought, that look from Fallows. That tone in his voice that cut all the others out and made him feel special. He could feel the others staring at him with envy and even a little fear. It made him feel powerful.

Fallows pointed ahead. "Whatever it is, it's about a mile straight through there. We run it at double-time, we should be there in six minutes. Let's go. Move your lazy asses."

There was no hesitation. The men started running full-speed along the dirt road. Fallows waited until they were all moving before he started. Within seconds he and Tim had passed them all and were leading the pack toward the house.

Paige bucked against the weight of the children, trying desperately to throw them off her arms and legs. But they merely giggled at the disturbance, as if they were riding a particularly fun mechanical ride outside the grocery store.

Wendy gripped both hands around the long knife's handle and lifted the serrated blade over head, ready to plunge it down into Paige's heart.

Paige twisted her body to the side, wiggling with such ferocity that her right foot slipped free from under Max, twelve, and Gail, nine. As they grabbed for the snaking foot, she coiled her leg back and snapped it straight into Max's face. He groaned as he flew back into Gail, both of them tumbling into another half-full bucket.

"Hold her, kids!" Wendy said, distracted just

long enough for Paige to kick her free foot into Wendy's chest. The blow staggered Wendy a few steps, but she recovered quickly enough to stab at the foot. The blade sawed through Paige's pant leg and sliced the ankle bone. The ankle pulsed with pain, but Paige kept kicking. Finally Max and Gail wrestled the leg to the ground, flopping their little bodies across it.

"Goodness," Wendy sighed, brushing a stray hair back into place and tugging her apron straight. She kneeled next to Paige and lifted the knife again.

The door to the pantry exploded open with such a violent force that it caught two of the children who'd been watching on the shoulders and hurled them into the wall. Eric stood in the doorway with his HK 93 held at waist level.

"Get away from her," he growled. "Move!"

Wendy dropped the knife and backed away, gathering her frightened children around her. She held her arms out, pushing them behind her, protecting them with her body as she imagined Ingrid Bergman might, or Katherine Hepburn. "Don't harm the children," she pleaded.

Eric ignored her. He gestured to Paige as she slowly pulled herself to her feet. "You OK?"

"Headache." That was all she seemed to be able to say for a moment. Then it burst out at once in rapid disbelief. "Eric, they were going to kill me and, Jesus . . ." She looked around the small room, her old secret hiding place. With the door open, the extra light revealed the hanging things more clearly. Legs, arms, torsos. Like a butcher shop. And there on the floor, spilled blood, scattered bones, and her former husband's severed head. "Cannibals. They're goddamn cannibals. Children." She shook her head, unable to continue. Then, in a sudden violent outburst, she snatched Wendy's knife from the floor and ran at the girl.

Wendy stuck out her chest and closed her eyes, offering herself up as sacrifice for the children's sake.

"Don't," Eric said.

Paige stood in front of the girl, her hand clutching the knife, her body shaking with rage. Finally she flung the knife to the floor. "Let's get out of here." Her voice was hollow, almost an echo.

Sound filtered in from outside. Men approaching.

"Drop it, kid!" a man shouted.

Another man laughed harshly. "What the fuck is this? Disneyland?"

Eric ducked out of the pantry, peeked out the kitchen door, saw nothing, slid along the side of the house and glanced around the corner.

Col. Dirk Fallows and his men were marching across the lawn. Next to Fallows, Tim. Eric noticed the Walther, his Walther, tucked in Tim's waistband.

Peter had managed to work the arrow free from his leg and was standing now, leaning on a couple of the children with one hand, holding his

211

machete in his other.

"What do you want?" Peter demanded.

"Want?" Fallows repeated with a smile. "We're just weary travellers looking for a couple friends of ours."

"Damn," Eric whispered to himself, spun and ran back to the kitchen door.

Paige was waiting there, silently threatening the children with the knife to keep them quiet. "What is it? What's going on?"

"No time," Eric said. "Let's go."

"OK, I'll grab my gun and the tapes."

Eric gripped her arm and yanked her out the door. "No time. They're coming in. Now."

"But the tapes—"

His fingers dug into her arm. "Forget them."

They ran full-speed across the back yard, Paige's ankle screaming from the deep cut Wendy had given her. They were into the woods just as some of Fallows's men burst into the house and herded Wendy and the children out into the yard with the others. One of them carried Paige's HK 93 with the laser scope.

"Hey, Colonel, looky here."

Fallows examined it, then glanced around, staring for a few seconds right through the trees where Eric and Paige were hiding. Eric knew he couldn't actually see him, but it was a chilling feeling anyway.

Fallows tossed the gun back to his soldier. "Looks like we got them while they were on the toilet. Took off with their pants still around their ankles." His eyes swept the grounds again.

"You want us to go after them?" one of the men asked.

Eric and Paige listened from their prone positions, exchanging looks.

"Not yet. Not until we see if they found what they were looking for. We'll tear this place apart first."

"Colonel!" a soldier shouted, stumbling out of the kitchen door, holding his stomach. "Jesus, Colonel." He doubled over and retched onto the ground.

"Christ, Bedlow," Fallows said with disgust.

Bedlow spat out what was left of his lunch and wiped the mess from his lips. "Cannibals, Colonel. These little bastards are cannibals. They got a fucking butcher shop in there. Arms, legs, everything. They eat *people*, for Chrissake."

"Really?" Fallows smiled with amusement as he looked the children over. "So you kids been chewing the fat, huh? Been biting the hand that feeds you?"

"What are you going to do?" Peter asked.

"Whatever we want," Fallows said. "So you and your brats just keep your mouths shut until we're done."

Peter stormed a few steps toward Fallows. "This is our home. You have no right to—"

Fallows tugged his Walther from its holster and shot Peter in the face. The bullet removed Peter's left cheek and a quarter of the back of his skull. Some of the younger children screamed and cried.

Most followed Wendy's example and just watched quietly.

"Shouldn't we do something?" Paige whispered.

"What?"

Paige thought about it, sighed. "Yeah."

But Eric wasn't concerned with what was going on as much as he was with Tim's reactions to it. He watched his son's face as Fallows blasted away Peter's face. There was the shock of the noise, but otherwise nothing. No reaction. Of all the dangers and life-threatening situations Eric had faced in his life, this frightened him the most. Come on, son, he begged silently, show me *something*.

Fallows left a man to guard the children and lead the others into the house. The loud sounds of the house being savaged, furniture being smashed, cupboards torn apart, drummed through the woods.

Eric nudged Paige. "Come on."

"Where?"

"Away from here."

"But the tapes. My father's tapes."

Eric shook his head. "Fallows has them now. It won't take him long to figure it out."

"Then what?"

Eric considered that for a moment. "If he found us here he must have gotten the info from Steve. That means he knows when the shuttle takes off again. He'll have to decide whether he's got enough time to come after us and still get to the shuttle in time." Eric pulled Paige to her feet and handed her the HK 93. He unslung the crossbow, cocked it, and fixed a bolt in the groove.

"What about them?" Paige asked, hooking a thumb over her shoulder. "What do you think those kids will do now that Peter's dead?"

"Eat him," Eric said.

20.

"My God, Eric, even that little girl—"

"Sarah."

"Yeah, Sarah. She was the one who hit me. Tried to kill me."

Eric brushed aside a branch and waited for Paige to walk through before letting it swing free. They'd retraced their trail for about five miles. Paige had babbled the whole time about their ordeal, trying to talk herself down, make some sense of it.

"It's like *Twilight Zone*, you know," she said. "Innocent faces invite you to dinner. Only you turn out to be the main course. Jesus."

"You've got to let it go, Paige," Eric said. He'd let her talk uninterrupted for the past forty-five minutes. Now he sensed she wanted some answers. He didn't have any, but he would try.

"But they're *kids*, damn it. Children. Where'd they learn to do something so horrible?"

"That's just it. They're too young to have a clear sense of it being all that horrible. All they know is that when you get hungry, you eat. Peter would have had to be a hell of a hunter to provide enough game for all of them to eat. And they don't look like they know much about gardening. So they ate the bodies that were lying around. Like that family Tracy and I saw earlier in a cabin, just before the shuttle landed. Some of these kids had the same symptoms, probably from eating the contaminated flesh."

"But why us?"

"Maybe they were afraid we'd tell others where they were. Maybe we just looked too tasty to let slip away."

"That's not funny."

"Sure it is. As funny as you're going to get here. You just arrived. Wait until you've been here awhile. You'll be slapping your knees at the strangest things."

She glared at him. "That's one delight I don't have to worry about. As soon as I get back to the *Columbia*, we're taking off. They had to do some fancy redesigning so it could take off on its own, and I don't intend to let their ingenuity go to waste. I just wish you'd let me go back for the tapes and my pack. Now I can't even contact Dr. Piedmont."

"They were already marching across the front lawn. There wasn't time to go back."

"Maybe," she said. "Or maybe you didn't want me to be able to contact the craft. Maybe you just want to stall me until you can get your son back."

"That's our deal, lady. I help you find your father's papers in exchange for Tim's passage. I kept my side of the bargain."

"But now Fallows has them."

Eric shrugged. "Not my problem. I found them, that's all I said I'd do."

"Fine," she spat. "But I'm heading straight back to the ship. If you and your son are there when we take off, we'll talk about it then."

"That could be too late."

"I promised to hold a seat open, not wait."

Eric grabbed her under the arm and spun her around. "There's still almost twenty-one hours left."

"Not if I get there sooner. And at this rate—" she glanced at her watch—"I'll be there in another two or three hours."

"Not if I don't lead you back."

"OK, add on another hour or two. I may not be Gertrude Girl Scout, but I've had survival navigation. I'll find my way."

Eric grinned. "Maybe."

Paige looked a little uncertain. "Look, Eric, I'm not trying to foul you or your boy up. I mean, you did save my life and everything. But I've got responsibilities too. With Steve gone we should have room for you. Maybe even squeeze on your lady friend. But we're not waiting around while that madman and his army come marching toward us, with you single-handedly trying to take your son away from him. You come back to the States with us, find another way back, maybe with some troops of your own. That's my final offer, and it's the best one you're going to get. Otherwise, I'm heading out on my own right now. So make up your mind."

Eric watched her pick up her gun and march away through the woods. He let her go.

Book Three:

THE THROAT OF WAR

Before mine eyes in opposition sits
Grim Death, my son and foe . . .

—Milton

21.

Fallows rigged the wires to the batteries and punched the Play button. Isolated piano notes staggered through the tinny speaker. After listening to it half a dozen times, he was able to correlate the notes to the letters and numbers of the code. Some code, he thought. But poor Dr. Lyons probably hadn't had time for anything too elaborate.

"Phelps, come here." He waved.

"Sure, Colonel." Phelps left the circle of men who were sitting in the garage of the Union 76 station, what was left of it. The garage part of the building was still pretty intact, complete with a yellow diesel Rabbit parked inside. Someone had long ago drained the oil and fuel from the car and from the station. The other half of the building, the one with the office containing the rack of local state maps and vending machines and bathrooms, had been sheared off when the ground split during the quake. A ragged fissure zigzagged along the ground as far as one could see in either direction. The half with the garage had sunk, leaving the other half of the station on the other side of a ten-foot crevice, eight feet higher.

"What's up, Colonel?" Phelps asked, absently scratching himself.

Fallows said, "Listen." He played the piano notes. "What's that sound like to you?"

Phelps continued scratching himself. "Shit, I dunno. Sounds like some dude don't know how to play the piano."

Fallows turned to Tim, who sat within arm's reach on the edge of the gas pump island, next to the unleaded. "What do you think, Tim? Some tone-deaf Beethoven?"

Tim listened again, though he'd heard it every time Fallows had played it. "No, there's a pattern, but it's not based on sound. Probably a code."

"A code, kid?" Phelps guffawed. "You been playin' with yourself too much."

"He's right, Phelps," Fallows said. "It's a code."

Phelps face crumpled. "Sure, Colonel, a code. But what for?"

"You can get back with the others now," Fallows said.

Phelps hesitated, fighting his anger and embarrassment, not wanting to say anything Fallows would make him regret. He wandered back to the rest of the men.

Fallows listened to the tape a few minutes longer. Mentally he transposed notes with corresponding numbers and letters. A gift, really. Perfect pitch. His piano teacher had fussed over young Dirk Fallows, encouraging the lad to develop his remarkable talent even further. "You could be great," Mr. Letweller had rhapsodized. "Perhaps among the best." But Dirk's mastery of the instrument had come so easily, as with many other things, he became bored with it. He wanted something more active, more exciting. Skydiving, hot-rodding, mountain climbing. Dirk Fallows's hair had turned completely white by the time he was eighteen; some joked it had burned out on all of Dirk's dangerous exploits. Doctors theorized it might have been a vitamin deficiency, a kind of birthmark.

He punched the Stop button. "We'll be there in a few hours, Tim. Give the men a chance to rest up first, then we march straight for that shuttle."

"What makes you think it will still be there? My father and that astronaut won't rest. They could be there and take off."

Fallows grinned. "I know your father pretty well. Better than you realize. She may want to get back and take off, but not your dad. He'll come back."

"For me," Tim said.

"For *me*," Fallows said. "I told you, if he'd wanted you, he'd have grabbed you by now."

Tim didn't say anything. He reached into his

pocket and fondled the thick bullet.

Fallows looked away, but still watched Tim. Good, the longer he kept the bullet, the more he'd lose his desire to use it. It would become more of a charm then. Fallows had seen the same brainwashing technique in Cambodia. Give the prisoner a small weapon, but within circumstances that make it suicidal to use it. The longer they don't use it, the more they convince themselves that there's a reason why they don't. That they don't really want to harm their captors. That, in fact, the captors trusted them with a weapon, so they must care. Loyalties become confused. Looking at Tim, Fallows realized it was only a matter of time.

Fallows smiled to himself. Soon he and Tim would be aboard the *Columbia* and on their way back to civilization. Part of him would miss this place. He liked its rawness, the potential to become anything. In time, maybe even a monarchy, a kingdom, with you-know-who playing the part of the wise king. His only regret was that he hadn't killed Eric. That desire was an ache deep inside him that was always there. Beating a reminder. But maybe this was even better. Yeah, leaving the island with Eric's son, and poor Daddy unable to follow, having to live the rest of his life here knowing his only son was being raised by his worst enemy. He chuckled to himself. Yes, that was even better than killing him, letting him slowly kill himself.

"Coming in, Colonel," Eli Palmer called

through the brush.

Fallows stood up, reached for his Walther. What was Palmer doing back here so soon? He was supposed to be stationed on the southeast perimeter keeping watch.

"Move it, bitch," Palmer said, stepping through the underbrush onto the road. He shoved Paige Lyons in the back with her own HK 93 and she stumbled face-forward into the buckled pavement. Shards of macadam dug into her palms and arms. Palmer kicked her buttocks. "Move your fucking ass before I blow it off."

Paige struggled to her knees, brushing off some of the pebbles that were embedded in her palm.

"Faster," Palmer barked, grabbing her blond ponytail in his fist and yanking her to her feet. Then he started running, dragging her after him. "Hup, hup, hup." He laughed.

Fallows was smiling, hands on his hips, as Palmer gave her a final rough tug on her hair.

"Found her sneaking through the woods about a mile south."

Fallows nodded. "Following the same trail they'd taken up."

"Just like you figured," Palmer said.

"Where's Ravensmith, Dr. Lyons?" Fallows asked politely.

Paige pecked at the pebbles in her hand, digging one large one out of her thumb. Blood swelled into the tiny hole. "I don't know."

Fallows's right hand lashed out and clamped around her throat, his thumb denting her windpipe. "Are you sure?"

Paige looked into Fallows's face for the first time and felt a tremor of terror as if her whole insides were suddenly shrinking. The eyes, so pale they reminded her of special contact lenses they use in the movies for vampires. The bristly white hair like a thicket of snow-covered thorns. The mouth, thin and sharp. If his lips were pressed against paper and he smiled, he would probably shred the paper. But even more than the physical features was the sense of energy. Relentless throbbing energy ready to flood and drown anybody around him.

She shook her head, unable to speak as his thumb dug deeper into her throat. "Don't . . . know," she finally croaked.

He released his grip.

Paige coughed twice and clutched her own throat, rubbing feeling back into it. "We argued," she explained. "I wanted to get back to the ship as quickly as possible and take off. He wanted to stay around here, try to get his son back."

Tim stood up.

Fallows's smile turned cruel. "Where is he now?"

"I don't know. I told him I wouldn't help him and we split up."

"He let you go, huh?" Fallows said skeptically. "Just like that?"

"He didn't want to," Paige said. "But his crossbow is no match for an HK 93."

Fallows studied her a moment. That ache

228

inside, the animal that gnawed at his guts every time he thought of Eric Ravensmith, was at it again. Worse than ever. There was still time. Time enough to find Ravensmith and still get to the shuttle. If he knew where to look. "Where did you split up? Exactly."

Paige shrugged. "I don't know exactly. Not too far from the house with those, uh, kids."

"Yes, them. Creators of the New California Diet. Well, they won't be dining out anymore."

"You killed them?" Disbelief.

"Of course. It's not wise to leave enemies behind, especially here."

Paige looked into Tim's eyes, but he stared at her without any expression.

"Now, Dr. Lyons," Fallows said. "Once more. Exactly where did you leave Eric?"

"I told you where. I can't be more exact."

"Do you know what direction he took when he left you?"

"South, I think."

He shook his head. "Why do I have trouble believing you, Dr. Lyons?"

"I'm telling you the truth."

"Perhaps. But then again, perhaps not. Only one way to be sure." He slid his knife from the sheath. "Palmer, take her into the garage and tie her across the hood of the Rabbit."

Palmer grinned. "Like a deer, you mean?"

"Arms and legs spread."

He licked his lips. "Naked?"

"Naturally."

Palmer grabbed Paige's ponytail again and dug the HK 93 into her back.

"But I told you the truth," Paige pleaded.

"You probably did," Fallows agreed. "But a little pain will help convince me." He followed behind them, tapping his knife in the palm of his hand.

22.

Eric listened to the screams as he cooked the last of the squirrel. The orange sky was draining into gray as the bright smear of the sun was replaced by the pale smear of the moon.

Another scream. Paige's husky voice stretched into a high shriek of horror.

He poked a stick at the squirrel brains as they cooked. They were not only edible, but they could be used to tan hides. That's what he liked about nature, it was so damned efficient. Nothing is wasted. The skin, tongue, heart, liver and kidneys—all edible. Even the cheek pads. The eyeballs contain a liquid that can be used for paints and dyes, or mixed with pitch to make a hard-setting glue. Behind the eyeball was a small

231

piece of tasty fat.

Paige's scream pierced the air like a sonic boom.

And then there's the blood. Rich with iron, salts and other nutrients. Makes a good stew or soup.

He tore a chunk of cooked meat from the squirrel's rib. Some hunters claimed squirrel tasted like chicken or rabbit. It didn't. It was more exotic than that, as if it had been seasoned with rare herbs.

"God, please," Paige cried. Her sobs bounced along the deep crevice and into Eric's ears as he sat barely a quarter mile away from the Union 76 station. But on the other side of the ten-foot cleft. The crevice was even wider further north, spanning almost twenty feet at one point. About a mile south, where he and Paige had crossed on the way up and he had crossed a few hours ago, the rift in the earth disappeared completely. He'd looked over the edge earlier, but there was nothing to see but endless dark. He'd thrown a rock over, but he'd never heard it hit bottom.

Paige cried out again, her voice hoarse from abuse. It was a long scream this time, maybe ten seconds. Eric could imagine what Fallows was doing. He'd seen it all before.

But he wasn't thinking about that now as he pulled off another strip of squirrel meat. He wasn't thinking about Paige. He was thinking about Tim. About the look on his face when Fallows had shot Peter in the head. The lack of expression, the missing cry of outrage. Was this the same boy who'd once accused Eric of murder for overwatering the Boston fern? The same young face but with hollow eyes and an indifferent mouth. Eric wondered if he looked as dispassionate as his Tim had, as he sat there eating squirrel and listening to Paige's screams.

23.

"You've got four hours," Fallows told them, his arm around Tim. "Four hours to track him down and bring him back to me."

"Alive?" Phelps asked.

"If possible."

The twelve men stood around Fallows checking their weapons. The torture of Paige Lyons hadn't taken more than fifteen or twenty minutes. She hadn't said anything new.

Fallows stooped down and drew a map in the dirt with his knife. Some of Paige's blood was still on the blade. "This ravine curves down here for another mile, then ends. Ravensmith could cross anywhere along here. It would take him too far out of his way to go any further south."

Palmer glanced over at the ravine that split the service station. "That's a ten-foot jump across, Colonel. Not to mention eight feet up. Only way to get to the other side from here would be to leap across and grab hold of the edge of the cliff there, then pull yourself up." He shook his head. "Hell of a chance."

"Believe me, one this man would take. Besides, the cliff levels out the further south you travel, so chances are he'll be down there somewhere, probably waiting for us to cross so he can start picking us off."

"With nothing but a fucking crossbow?" Phelps scoffed.

Fallows smiled. "How's he done so far?"

The men exchanged nervous glances.

"One other thing," Fallows said. "If you don't find him, don't come back. Ever."

"We'll find him, Colonel," Phelps said. "Don't worry."

Fallows turned around and guided Tim away.

"All right," Phelps snapped, "let's move out."

The men double-timed down the road, their heavy boots pounding like a team of horses.

Fallows deployed the remaining men to positions deeper in the woods. "Anything moves," he warned, "blast it. This is one time I don't care if you waste bullets."

Tim said, "What about her? The lady astronaut?"

Fallows looked over his shoulder into the darkening garage. Paige was still tied across the hood of the Rabbit. Her clothes lay in a pile next to the car. "What about her?"

"What are you going to do with her?"

"What do you think?"

"Kill her."

Fallows grinned. "Bingo. But not yet. Not until we see if my men can find good ole Eric. Besides, we might need her to bargain our way aboard the shuttle."

This was the first Tim had heard anything about going aboard the craft. "What do you mean?"

Fallows lowered his voice, even though he and Tim were the only ones left in camp. "I'm taking you out of here, kid. I mean off this crazy island." He walked over to the campfire they'd built on the far side of the garage.

Tim followed eagerly. "I don't get it."

"I told you before, Tim, the time would come when you'd see who really had your best interests at heart. Your dad wasn't able to protect your mom or sister. Or you. And for all his chest-beating, has he even come close to getting you back? Weren't we the ones who chased after him? Huh?"

Tim didn't say anything.

Fallows tossed a log onto the fire. Sparks burst up into a tiny fireworks display. "Come on, we'll get some more wood. We've got a four-hour wait."

They walked along the chewed-up pavement, gathering dried branches from the side of the road. Fallows spoke as they walked, his tone easy and caring, a stiff imitation of Eric's. "But when I promise something, Tim, I deliver. You and I are going to get off this island, courtesy of NASA."

Tim picked up a few small branches.

"And once we get back, I'll take care of you, just like I am now."

Fallows let Tim think it over as they continued to stroll along the road, adding wood to their armloads. He knew the anguish going on in Tim's mind now, but he also knew how it would all be resolved. The walk in the woods away from the woman's tortured whimpering, the compassionate tone so like Eric's, and most important, the hope of freedom. There was only one way Tim could go.

It was all working out so perfectly. If his men found Eric, they'd bring him back broken and humiliated. Or dead. Either way, Fallows won. If they didn't find him, Fallows would kill the men he had left and use the tapes to bargain his passage back to the States.

The woman's arrival had only delayed him a few hours. But it was worth it if he could find Eric. Maybe he wouldn't kill Eric, just mutilate him somehow, cut off his hands or feet, or maybe one of each. Then leave him here to contemplate the life his son would be having with Fallows as his parent. That thought made the small gnawing inside him go away. Yes, death was too sudden, too final.

Fortunately the woman had been able to confirm his own conclusions about the tapes. He'd played them for her while he'd tortured her, the staccato notes echoing around the garage while she screamed. Yes, it had been a stroke of luck finding her wandering nearby. He stopped in the middle of the road. Maybe too lucky. Eric must have known they'd capture her. Yet he let her go.

"Damn," he cried, throwing the wood down.

"What?" Tim asked.

"That son of a bitch!" Fallows pulled his Walther from his holster and began running back to the service station.

Tim followed, fumbling in his pocket for the single 9mm bullet.

Eric ran as fast as he could, straight for the ravine. As his right foot slapped the ground only six inches from the edge, he pushed off, his feet bicycling through the air over the endless drop below him. The weight of the crossbow on his back made him a little nervous, but once he was airborne, he forgot about it. He forgot about everything except how good the ground would feel beneath his feet. He pictured himself missing, tottering on the far edge, slipping backwards, bouncing down against the dirt and rock walls. . . .

His feet bumped dirt and he pitched himself forward like a runner diving for home plate. He was safe. About a hundred yards away he could see the outline of the garage backlit by the campfire. He had waited until he'd seen where Fallows dispatched the guards. That Fallows had then led Tim away had been a bonus.

Eric found the first guard north of the Union 76 station, crouching behind some burned bushes that had obviously been caught in a brush fire. The guard was maybe thirty-five with a red checkered bandanna tied over his head. A gold cross dangled from one ear.

Eric sneaked up behind him as the guard's head swung back and forth, scanning the dark woods. Eric threw his arm around the guard's head, pressing his forearm into the man's mouth to prevent him from crying out. With his right hand, he tried to dig his knife into the man's throat. But the guard used his powerful neck muscles to force his chin down, making it hard for Eric to find his target. Instead he plunged the blade into the man's heart. The cries of anguish were muffled against Eric's forearm as the guard sagged to the ground. Eric picked up the dead man's carbine and trekked quietly toward the garage.

The dead guard was the closest one to the garage, and with him out of the way, Eric figured he had a chance. Free Paige, get her across the ravine to safety, then eliminate the other guards one by one while the rest of the troops were out looking for him. And finally, Fallows.

He crawled along the wall of the garage, looked around, then ducked inside. The fire from the other side of the wall cast a flickering light through the dirty window. A large sign against the back wall said: OUR INSURANCE FORBIDS CUSTOMERS INSIDE GARAGE. Next to that was another sign: PLEASE DON'T ASK TO USE OUR TOOLS.

Eric stooped between the yellow Rabbit and the wall and crab-walked to the front of the car. Paige was still stretched out on the hood. One eye was swollen shut, but she saw him with the other.

"What . . . kept you?" she said slowly, her lip split in front.

Eric tried not to look at her as he untied her wrists. He'd already seen enough. The dozens of little cuts across her body, the long S that started between her breasts and curved down to her pubic hair. There was blood dripping down her hips.

When he'd finished untying her he helped her dress. "No time," he said, throwing away her bra and panties. "Just the basics." Finally, with painful, halting movements, she was dressed. He handed her the carbine. "Let's get you out of here."

"Aren't you going to say something?"

"What?"

She looked at him with her good eye. A sliver of white shone under the swollen eye. "Say it, damn it!"

"All right. I told you so. Better?"

"Damn right, that's better," she slurred. "You warned me not to go out on my own. I didn't

240

listen. Now you're saving my life for the second time. You at least owe me an I-told-you-so."

"Not yet, lady. Not until you see what's next." He steadied her with his arm around her waist, half-carrying her toward the door.

"The tapes!" she said. "Over there!"

Eric leaned her against the Rabbit's hatchback and ran back to the workbench. The cassette player was there. He popped the cassette out and grabbed the one lying next to it, stuck them both in his shirt pocket. When he returned to help Paige, she waved him away. "I'm OK." She shuffled forward a few steps to demonstrate. "See?"

Eric lead her outside. "Listen, Paige, there's only time to do this once. I'm going to jump across that ravine. Then you're going to jump."

She laughed hoarsely. "There's got to be an easier way to kill me, Eric."

"I'm serious."

She shook her head. "I'll never make it. Maybe if I had a couple days' sleep and a few hours' practice. But not now, not this way."

"No choice, Paige. It's the only way you'll be safe if I don't make it back. Then at least you have a chance of getting back to the shuttle in time."

"The ravine's not the problem. I can probably jump that. But that damn cliff. It's too high, Eric. And too dark."

"Don't worry." He smiled. "I'll catch you."

She gave him a long, steady look. Finally she shrugged. "Sure, why not?"

Eric paced out the distance first, then ran it, pushing off the edge, reaching both arms straight up to grab hold of anything. Just like all those times he'd tried to make a slam dunk back when he played varsity basketball. Only he'd never quite been able to do it. He'd bounced a few off the rim, though. Close. Only this time, close wasn't going to be good enough. His leap was better than he'd anticipated. Both arms and shoulders were above the edge of the cliff and he managed to wrap his fists around the thick bush he'd been aiming for. Quickly he pulled himself up.

He waved at Paige. She walked up to the edge of the ravine and looked down. "I'm glad my other eye can't see," she said, "otherwise I'd be scared."

"Throw the gun first."

She swung the rifle back with both hands like someone giving the heave-ho, and flung it up into the air. But not high enough. Eric grabbed for it, but the gun was a foot too low. It struck the side of the cliff and dropped into the ravine, clattering noisily as it fell.

"Hurry," Eric urged.

"I hope you can catch better than that this time," she said as she backed up. She took a deep breath, tried to block out the pains that criss-crossed her body, and leaned over in the runner's start she'd learned in college. She leaned on her fingers, her butt high in the air, but she couldn't move.

"Come on," Eric said.

"I can't," she said softly to herself. "I can't make it."

And then she heard the pounding footsteps behind her and she knew she had no choice. She sprinted forward toward the dark ravine.

Fallows fired three shots into the air. "Leyson! Driscol! Rendall!" he shouted. *"Come here!"*

He watched Paige Lyons dashing for the ravine and saw Eric poised to catch her. He might be able to pick off one or both, but he was certain one of them had the tapes. And he didn't know which one. If he shot either of them right now, they were liable to go plunging right into the ravine, taking the tapes, his flight ticket aboard the shuttle, with them.

No rush. Soon she'd either be across or not. If not, well, he'd come up with something else. But if she made it, his men would be here soon anyway. Together they'd be able to finish both of them off.

Paige pushed off from the ground much too early, she realized immediately. Instead of waiting until she'd reached the edge, she'd panicked and started jumping at least two feet too soon. That meant she had to jump an extra two feet. She felt like she was all arms and legs as she floated through the air, the way she felt when she was a gawky twelve-year-old leaping from the high dive for the first time on a double dare from Rodney Belson.

She could see Eric through her good eye. He was stretched out on the ground, his feet anchored around some thick bush. For a moment they were face-level. But then she started dropping, and she was only a little more than halfway across. Her heart expanded until she was sure it was crushing the other internal organs. She forgot how to breathe. She began to fall, her hands straight over her head.

Eric snagged one of those hands, clamping her wrist in his fist. She knocked into the side of the cliff, scraping a few inches of skin from her forehead. Her weight dragged him a few inches over the edge of the cliff. But he had her, of that he was sure. He reeled her in, slowly pulling her up until she could crawl free from the edge.

Then he dove for his crossbow.

With both of them safe, Fallows lowered his Walther's sights on Eric's chest while Eric was busy cocking his crossbow. "Don't bother, Eric me boy," Fallows said under his breath as he tightened his finger around the trigger.

But a familiar sound behind him made him spin around in time to find Tim thumbing the single bullet into the clip and slamming the clip into the handle. Tim shoved the Walther into Fallows's face and fired.

Fallows had started dropping the moment he'd

recognized the sound. That instinct saved his life. Tim's bullet whipped by Fallows's temple with less than an inch to spare. But the powder flash scorched Fallows's eyes and he dropped to his knees rubbing them. "Fucking bastard!" he shouted. *"I could have saved you!"*

Tim stood over Fallows, trying to decide whether or not to wrestle the gun from his hands and finish him off.

Eric watched the scene from across the ravine, knowing what Tim was thinking. And knowing that Tim wouldn't have a chance. Even blind, Fallows could kill Tim instantly if he got his hands on him. He could kill Fallows himself with a shot of the crossbow.

He heard the rustling of brush, the sound of men running.

There wasn't time to kill Fallows and try to save Tim. It had to be one or the other. He didn't hesitate.

"Grab my legs," he ordered Paige. "Hold tight." He cupped his hands around his mouth and shouted to Tim. "Run, Tim. Run, son, I'll catch you."

Tim looked at his father, hesitated. Even now he remembered the things Fallows had said about his father. They couldn't be true, he felt that inside. But still, he hesitated.

The sound of Fallows's men was louder.

Fallows staggered to his feet, still rubbing his eyes with the heels of his palms.

"Run, Tim!" Eric called again.

And Tim ran. Hard and fast and with tears in his eyes as each step brought him closer to his father.

A shot cracked the air and Tim felt something bump the back of his thigh. Felt the leg fold under him. Felt himself tumbling toward the edge of the ravine.

"Timmmm!" his father screamed.

Tim dug into the ground, despite his wounded right leg. He stopped rolling a good ten feet from the edge of the cliff. He looked over his shoulder and saw Fallows squinting through one eye, holding the smoking Walther. "He's mine, Eric. My son now!"

Behind Fallows his men emerged from the woods, their M-16s and shotguns lowered for action.

Eric saw it was hopeless. He couldn't save Tim. Not this time. It would be all he could do to get himself and Paige out alive. He looked down at his son's dirty face, saw the blood seeping from his leg. The pain contorting his young face. And that look in his eyes, the look of abandonment. That look lodged in Eric's heart like a splinter.

Fallows and his men opened fire.

"Stay down," Eric said to Paige. "At this angle they can't hit us as long as we stay flat." Their bellies to the ground, Eric and Paige crawled away.

Behind him, Eric heard Tim's cry: *"Father!"*

When they were safely in the woods, Paige laid her hand on Eric's arm. "Eric."

"With Fallows and Tim wounded, we'll easily beat them back to your plane."

"Eric," she repeated. There were tears in her eyes.

Eric walked away. "Don't say anything, OK? Anything."

24.

"Christ, Paige!" was all Bart Piedmont could say as he and Daryl Budd carried her up into the belly of the *Columbia.*

Eric tagged behind them while Phil La Porte kept guard outside.

Tracy was waiting outside, hobbling about pretty spryly on her bad leg. Piedmont had put a real cast on the leg and she got about with a cane someone had cut for her from a branch. Tracy looked at both of them. "You're sure hell on women, Eric."

Paige laughed, winced from her split lip. "We were fine until he wanted to dance. The man's just too clumsy."

Tracy and Paige laughed together, one of those shared womanly laughs that Eric didn't pretend to understand. He just smiled at them, pleased they were able to find something to laugh about.

"How secure are we, sir?" Daryl Budd, all business, asked. Eric had to admire the guy's sense of duty.

"We've got a couple hours on them, I'd say. Maybe three hours, but I wouldn't want to bet on it. You'd better take off before then."

"Right, sir."

"What the hell happened out there?" Bart Piedmont demanded. "Did you find your father, Paige?"

Paige told the whole story, carefully, precisely. Eric marvelled at her recall of details and even dialogue.

As Paige spoke, Tracy put her arms around Eric and held him. She didn't have to hear the story to know what had happened. Eric was back, but Tim wasn't. That's all that mattered. At least Tim was still alive, but then so was Fallows.

Bart Piedmont listened as he tended Paige's wounds, cleaning and dressing her face. He could see the blood where it had seeped through her clothes. "Any other wounds I should take a look at?"

Paige brushed him away. "Not until you've at least bought me dinner."

"That can be arranged."

She stood up slowly. "Get this thing ready to take off, Bart."

"Aye, aye, Captain Kirk." He mock saluted. He turned to Eric and Tracy and smiled. "Fasten yourselves in, folks. We wouldn't want any of our passengers getting hurt."

Tracy knew what Eric would say, so she said it for him. "Thanks, Bart. Really. But we'll have to wait for the next train. There's still one passenger we've got to find."

"Tracy—" Bart started.

"Hey, I've already seen the in-flight movie." Tracy reached for her backpack. "See, I told you it was smart to pack this thing up this morning, just in case." She grabbed one of the HK 93s. "And this makes a nice little going-away present."

"Except that you're not going anywhere," Eric said. He took the pack and gun from her.

"What are you talking about? Tim's still out there."

"Yes, and I'm going after him. Only I'm going alone this time."

"Like hell!" she said.

He smiled, stroked her cheek with his finger-tips. "Listen, Tracy. I appreciate what you're trying to do. And I'm going to miss you, *really* miss you. But this is no good with you limping around this island forever. It's not going to do either of us any good."

Tracy stared into his eyes for a minute without speaking. When she did, her voice fought against sobbing. "I wish I could be braver, Eric. I wish I could say to hell with safety and the mainland. I'll stay here forever if that's how long it takes." She swallowed. "But I can't. I want to go back. I do. And I want you to come with me. Only I know you won't."

Eric leaned over and kissed her on the lips. It

was a light, almost chaste kiss, yet there was an energy there that transcended their past passions and touched an even deeper friendship.

Eric slung the pack over his shoulder and started for the ladder. "Hope there's some clean underwear in here."

"There is," Tracy said through her tears, "mine."

Eric laughed as he stepped onto the ladder.

"If you give me a couple of minutes to throw some things together," Paige said, "you can escort me out of here."

"What?" everyone said at once.

"Are you crazy?" Daryl Budd asked, then remembered his position and added, "ma'am."

"Paige, listen to me," Bart Piedmont said, his voice quietly calm. "You're in shock, some kind of delayed stress syndrome. You don't know what you're doing."

"Sure I do, Bart. I'm packing a few basic necessities and getting out of here."

"Listen to him, Paige," Eric said. "What just happened out there, that's only the beginning."

"Don't patronize me, Eric. I learn fast. I can imagine what else goes on out there. Oh, and don't think I'll be traveling with you, if that's what you're worried about. I'm strictly on my own. I'm going to find my father."

"Paige!" Bart pleaded, his voice no longer calm. "That's insane. He's probably dead. Those kids, those cannibal kids probably killed him. Or ate him like poor Steve."

Paige walked about the deck gathering things

251

and stuffing them into a nylon backpack. "I don't think so, Bart. He may be dead, but I don't think those kids knew him. I really don't. Something else happened to him, and that may mean he's alive."

"Jesus, Paige," Bart said. "Why? Why mess around with this now? After all this time?"

She nodded at Eric. "How come you don't ask him why he's going back out? Because he's a man and expected to look out for his family?"

"Come on, Paige, this is no time for Joan of Arc feminism. I don't deserve that crap."

"You're right, Bart. I'm sorry. I guess the only good reason I can give for going is that I think Dad would do it for me. The worst part about it is that it had never even occurred to me to *try* before today. For that, I'm ashamed."

Bart continued to plead as Paige stuffed her backpack. But even he realized it was no use after a while. He tried to force her stay by gunpoint, but she merely smiled and kissed him on the cheek.

Outside the ship, Daryl Budd made sure the others were aboard before climbing onto the ladder himself. He took one step, turned, and said to Eric, "Sir?"

"Yes?"

"The tapes." He held out his hand.

Eric smiled, handed the tapes over. Budd pocketed them. "Sir?"

"Yes?"

Budd reached down under his jacket and yanked the silver chain from around his neck. A silver Mickey Mouse dangled from the end. "It's not religious or anything. My girlfriend gave it to me for our second anniversary of going steady. Like I said, it's not religious, not like a charm or anything. No big deal." He shrugged, not sure what he was trying to say. "I dunno, I just know I'd like it if you took it. It couldn't hurt, huh?" He handed it to Eric.

"You think I'm nuts, too, don't you?" Paige asked.

"Yup."

"You think I should've gone back?"

"Uh-huh."

They stood on the edge of the dark runway and watched the *Columbia* rip along the pavement. Portable strobe lights had been set along the runway by Budd and La Porte and they blinked long after the plane disappeared into the dense Halo.

"Do you think those kids killed my father?"

"Nope."

"Then he might still be alive?"

"Maybe."

"But you still think I'm nuts."

"Yup."

She thought about that for a moment. "But you could have gone back. You didn't. You stayed too. How do you explain that?"

"Easy," he said. "I'm nuts too."

They found a secluded place to spend the night. Eric cooked a rabbit while Paige piled leaves into a soft bed. They sat next to the fire and talked.

Later they stripped naked and crawled into Paige's NASA sleeping bag. They made love twice. The first time Eric was careful because of Paige's wounds. The second time, Paige took control. Afterwards they slept holding each other close.

In the morning, they ate some leftover rabbit and tea and hardly talked at all. When it was over, they buried the fire, kissed, and said goodbye.

"See you." Paige waved as she headed south.

"Probably," Eric said, heading north.

THE SURVIVALIST SERIES
by Jerry Ahern

#3: THE QUEST   (851, $2.50)
Not even a deadly game of intrigue within the Soviet High Command, and a highly placed traitor in the U.S. government can deter Rourke from continuing his desperate search for his family.

#4: THE DOOMSAYER   (893, $2.50)
The most massive earthquake in history is only hours away, and Communist-Cuban troops, Soviet-Cuban rivalry, and a traitor in the inner circle of U.S. II block Rourke's path.

#5: THE WEB   (1145, $2.50)
Blizzards rage around Rourke as he picks up the trail of his family and is forced to take shelter in a strangely quiet Tennessee valley town. But the quiet isn't going to last for long!

#6: THE SAVAGE HORDE   (1243, $2.50)
Rourke's search gets sidetracked when he's forced to help a military unit locate a cache of eighty megaton warhead missiles hidden on the New West Coast—and accessible only by submarine!

#7: THE PROPHET   (1339, $2.50)
As six nuclear missiles are poised to start the ultimate conflagration, Rourke's constant quest becomes a desperate mission to save both his family and all humanity from being blasted into extinction!

#8: THE END IS COMING   (1374, $2.50)
Rourke must smash through Russian patrols and cut to the heart of a KGB plot that could spawn a lasting legacy of evil. And when the sky bursts into flames, consuming every living being on the planet, it will be the ultimate test for THE SURVIVALIST.

Available wherever paperbacks are sold, or order direct from the Publisher. Send cover price plus 50¢ per copy for mailing and handling to Zebra Books, Dept. 1437, 475 Park Avenue South, New York, N.Y. 10016. DO NOT SEND CASH.

THE SAIGON COMMANDOS SERIES
by Jonathan Cain

#2: CODE ZERO: SHOTS FIRED (1329, $2.50)

When a phantom chopper pounces on Sergeant Mark Stryker and his men of the 716th, bloody havoc follows. And the sight of the carnage nearly breaks Stryker's control. He will make the enemy pay; they will face his SAIGON COMMANDOS!

#4: CHERRY-BOY BODY BAG (1407, $2.50)

Blood flows in the streets of Saigon when Sergeant Mark Stryker's MPs become targets for a deadly sniper. Surrounded by rookies, Stryker must somehow stop a Cong sympathizer from blowing up a commercial airliner—without being blown away by the crazed sniper!

#5: BOONIE-RAT BODY BURNING (1441, $2.50)

Someone's torching GIs in a hellhole known as Fire Alley and Sergeant Stryker and his MPs are in on the manhunt. To top it all off, Stryker's got to keep the lid on the hustlers, deserters, and Cong sympathizers who make his beat the toughest in the world!

#6: DI DI MAU OR DIE (1493, $2.50)

The slaughter of a U.S. payroll convoy means it's up to Sergeant Stryker and his men to take on the Vietnamese mercenaries the only way they know how: with no mercy and with M-16s on full automatic!

#7: SAC MAU, VICTOR CHARLIE (1574, $2.50)

Stryker's war cops, ordered to provide security for a movie being shot on location in Saigon, are suddenly out in the open and easy targets. From that moment on it's Lights! Camera! Bloodshed!

Available wherever paperbacks are sold, or order direct from the Publisher. Send cover price plus 50¢ per copy for mailing and handling to Zebra Books, Dept. 1437, 475 Park Avenue South, New York, N.Y. 10016. DO NOT SEND CASH.